CAFÉ CAROLINA AND OTHER STORIES

CAFÉ CAROLINA AND OTHER STORIES

Jefferson Flanders

Munroe Hill Press
Lexington, Massachusetts

CAFÉ CAROLINA AND OTHER STORIES

Cover photo by Robert Matthews © 2010

Munroe Hill Press, Lexington, Massachusetts

ISBN: 978-0988784024

eISBN: 978-0988784048

Printed in the United States of America

For Maisie

Contents

Introduction

These twelve stories were written over the past three decades. Many were composed late at night, after work and family responsibilities had been met.

They reflect, in part, aspects of the people and places encountered along my way. And the rest, the transformation of experience into story, comes from the imagination.

"Café Carolina," the first story in this collection, was inspired by the song "Maggie's Dream" by Dave Loggins and Lisa Silver.

"Something More Than This" borrows its title from a song written by Julie Flanders and Emil Adler on the October Project album *Falling Farther In*.

A poem by Robinson Jeffers, "The Extraordinary Patience of Things," suggested the story of the same name.

I've greatly benefited from the critical reading of these stories by John Griffin, Linda Salisbury, Glenn Speer, Carl Flanders, and Julie Flanders and from their perceptive editorial suggestions.

– JF

December 2012

1

1

Café Carolina

They certainly weren't locals. Clearly they were out-of-towners, outsiders, although Evelyn wouldn't agree with any of Gina's other conjectures about the couple. But she agreed that they were out of place. They dressed too well, and they spoke too softly for a place like the Café Carolina.

As a rule, the Carolina didn't attract too many strangers. An occasional family of tourists, lost en route to Asheville, might stop for lunch and directions, or a traveling salesman prospecting for new leads might linger for a cup of coffee, but for the most part, the Café drew only familiar faces. There were the townspeople and the farmers and, of course, the good 'ole boys, as Evelyn called the morning cluster of coffee drinkers in baseball caps at the front counter.

This couple was different. No one had seen them before, and with their TV soap opera good looks it was impossible not to notice them. The mystery pair definitely had romance on their minds, as far as Gina could tell. That the two were lovers was one of Gina's initial hunches, and as much as Evelyn resisted the idea, she couldn't offer a better, or more believable, explanation for their sudden appearance in the last booth in the back, in Gina's service area, on the very cold second Monday of February, and then every Monday morning after that.

"We don't know that they're a couple," Evelyn maintained. "Not in that way. You're jumping to conclusions, Gina."

"I've got a sixth sense about this," Gina told her. "I trust my instincts."

"We don't know who they are. We don't know their names or where they're from. They could be brother and sister, for all we know."

Gina hooted in delight at that. "Brother and sister! If a brother and sister look at each other that way, then it's time to call the police. Even over in Yancey County they'd figure it was incest. They're definitely not brother and sister, or even kissing cousins. They're in love, trust me. I see all the signs of it."

"They're sitting in your booth. So you have an advantage. I haven't seen them up close like you have. From across the room, it looks like they could be family members. They've got the same coloring, and they're both tall."

"They say that when you are really in love with someone, you start to look like them. Sort of a romantic body language or mirror image."

"Are they wearing wedding rings?" Evelyn asked. "That'd tell us something."

"Actually, she is," Gina said. "He isn't. I checked out their hands the first time I had them in the booth."

"So maybe they are married. To each other. Lots of men don't like wearing a ring."

"They may be married, but I'd bet it's not to each other."

"How can you say that?"

"Because they don't look at each other the way married people do. At least not most married people, 'specially after they've been married for a while."

"So you think they're cheating?"

Gina nodded her head slowly. "I think that's a more than likely explanation for why they're meeting here, coming here for coffee, picking the booth in the back. They can't chance anywhere near their own hometown. I don't think they want anyone they know spotting them together. Too risky."

"I don't like to think the worst," Evelyn said. Gina didn't believe that; she had always found Evelyn narrow and judgmental.

"There's one other thing. They arrived separately the last few times. A few minutes apart. One waiting for the other. Which means they drove here in different cars."

"You're guessing," Evelyn said. "You don't know, for sure."

"Maybe I do have an active imagination." Gina paused. She didn't like to concede anything to Evelyn. "But it passes the time. Look at it this way—we wouldn't be standing here discussing them if I didn't have an imagination. We'd go on about our business without anything to keep our minds active. How boring would that be?"

Evelyn had always disapproved of what she viewed as Gina's wild flights of fancy. Evelyn had little imagination herself, and she was married to the dullest man in North Carolina, if not in the country, from what Gina could tell.

"Your stories are going to bring bad luck," Evelyn said. "You'll jinx someone. You really shouldn't make up stuff. Think about the times in the past you've been flat wrong."

"I've been right, too. Some of my hunches have been pretty close to the mark."

"Like the FBI agent?"

Gina had been wrong on that. A year before she had been convinced that a clean-cut visitor to the Café was an FBI agent looking for traces of Tommy Benton. Benton, a local bookkeeper, had embezzled close to $100,000 from the Ag Co-op before disappearing from town. But Gina was wrong. The man turned out to be a college football coach passing through town to scout a flashy running back at the regional high school. But Gina had been right on other occasions. She was the first to guess that Sharon Gibson was pregnant, that Steve Cropper was sick with cancer, and that Leslie Raye's marriage was in deep trouble (although Evelyn claimed that Frank Raye had always had a roving eye, even in the early days of his marriage to Leslie).

She ignored Evelyn's criticism, though, because the new couple intrigued her in ways she didn't quite understand. She found herself looking forward to Mondays and their mid-morning appearance. They arrived at the Café usually around ten o'clock, well after the breakfast rush. They stayed for almost two hours. Their custom was to leave the Carolina right before lunch, between 11:45 and noon. Early on Mondays Gina discouraged other customers from sitting in the back booth because she didn't want the couple to find it occupied and sit elsewhere, possibly outside her area of the floor.

Saving the booth for them meant she lost some tips. And the couple didn't order much, but Gina didn't care. When they did have food it was just a bowl of soup, or a side of toast, or an occasional cheese omelet for the man. Mostly they drank coffee and talked in hushed voices.

"They ain't hungry for my cooking," said Shep rudely after Gina once gave him the couple's order for buttered toast. Earlier, he'd stepped out of the kitchen on a pretext so he could see the couple he'd heard the waitresses talking about. "They're hungry for something else."

"Your mind is in the gutter," Gina said.

"Forbidden fruit," he said, baring his strong white front teeth in a wolfish grin. "They're hungry for forbidden fruit."

"They certainly wouldn't be hungry for your slop," said Evelyn, who was waiting for an order. "It's no wonder we run through so much ketchup. The customers are smothering what we serve in Heinz, and I don't blame them."

"Just because you're always horny doesn't mean everyone else is," Gina said.

"We're all horny," Shep said with certainty. "You two just won't admit it. What did that scientific study show? We all think about sex every nine seconds. Every nine seconds."

"Subtract the time when I have to look at you," Evelyn said.

In response, Shep gave them another grin, a leering one, and began singing an off-key chorus from the song "Afternoon Delight." Gina thought about the couple's obvious passion for each other and she blushed. Somehow it seemed wrong for Shep to mock them, to make their situation tawdry and cheap when she was certain that wasn't the case.

Normally, Shep's antics didn't bother her. She had always considered him a sad little man. Shep had been to culinary school in Poughkeepsie, New York and fancied himself a chef. He claimed that he had worked in the fanciest restaurants in Manhattan before tiring of big city life. He had turned up at the Café Carolina without explanation one day, impressed the owner, Gil Gaskins, and had been hired on the spot. Shep was missing half of a finger on his right hand, the ring finger, but according to Evelyn, who had worked at the Carolina several years longer than Gina, no one at Café Carolina had ever learned how he lost it.

After working with him for a while, Gina had concluded that Shep compensated for his lack of stature with a smart mouth. He was brighter than most people gave him credit for. Evelyn had never warmed up to Shep. She saw only the strutting bantamweight with a shaved-bald head and an immaculate white chef's blouse. Evelyn tried to avoid him. Shep knew it and dogged her with vulgar comments every chance he got.

Evelyn didn't share Gina's protectiveness towards the couple, but she was curious, nonetheless. She encouraged Gina to learn more.

"Why don't you try talking to them?" she suggested. "Not in a nosey way, but I'll bet you could find out more. Just ask them where they are from. That would be a quick way to maybe figure out what they're up to."

"I'm not going to be that rude," Gina responded. "It's none of my business. It's none of yours either."

Gina didn't want to scare them off. She was afraid too many questions would unsettle the couple and encourage them to find another place to meet. On her own, however, she began a serious study of the couple. She watched their faces when they talked. She observed their body language; how often they laughed, how often their hands touched. She noted their habits. They both liked coffee: he drank his black, she ordered decaffeinated with half-and-half and Sweet and Low.

She quickly learned their first names from overhearing their conversation. The man's name was Pierce, which somehow seemed to fit him. He addressed the woman as Amanda, and once or twice, Gina heard him call her Mandy. The woman seemed anxious; she was always looking around, one eye on the front door. Either she was high strung by nature, or she felt guilty, Gina decided. Whatever the case, it didn't diminish her attractiveness. Her clothes seemed to fit her as if they'd been tailored, even her blue jeans. She had a simple elegance about her, even though she rarely wore much jewelry or make-up.

Gina found herself glaring at some of the regular customers, especially the men, when they spent too much time glancing back at the last booth. Gina noticed that Amanda began sitting with her back to the rest of the restaurant, discouraging any male attention, even though that meant she couldn't watch the front door. Gina respected her more for that.

She wondered how long they had been seeing each other. Were their visits to the Carolina the opening phase in a dawning love affair? Or had it been going on for a while? How long had they known each other? Had they waited for years to act on their feelings? Did they have to sneak away to be together? What excuses did they have to make, or what lies did they have to tell? Was the Carolina their only stop Monday mornings, or did they find their way to a motel later and act on their obvious infatuation?

She didn't share all that she knew, or what she had discovered, with Evelyn or Shep. She had overheard the couple on several occasions and knew that all was not well between them, that they were struggling with something. Once she caught bits and pieces of an argument.

"This is impossible," Amanda had said. Her hushed voice had an intensity that was painful to hear. Gina was pouring coffee for a customer in the adjacent booth and kept her back to them. Amanda had a softer accent than Pierce. Her voice made Gina think of family friends from Leesburg, Virginia.

"Can't you be patient?" Pierce asked. "Just a little patience."

"Why?" she asked. "What damn difference will it make?"

"Don't think that way."

"Why not? What's the point of this, Pierce? Can you tell me?"

By then Gina had finished with coffee for the nearby booth and had to move away, back to the kitchen, and so she missed the end of the conversation.

She ached for the elegant couple and hoped they could work out whatever it was that was troubling them. Gina could see the real tenderness between them; the way they looked at each, like no one else was around, in their own world in the last booth of the Carolina. She only wished she might have experienced such tenderness, but hers had been a life without much opportunity for that. She was surprised that she cared so much about a pair of strangers, although she felt that she knew them. It bothered her when things didn't go well, like the one time she had spotted Amanda crying.

It happened immediately after Pierce had left the restaurant. Gina hadn't noticed anything out of the ordinary that morning. Her mystery couple had seemed happy to sit and sip their coffee and talk. But after Pierce's departure, Amanda sat in the booth by herself and cried for close to five minutes. She tried to hide her face, dabbing at her cheeks with paper napkins from the dispenser on the table. Gina kept a respectful distance, but all the while, she stayed close because she was curious. She wished she could go over to the booth, sit next to Amanda, and comfort her. Finally the woman rose to her feet, her head down, and left the Carolina quickly, avoiding any eye contact.

As the weeks passed, Gina's proprietary feelings about the couple—her couple—grew. She hungered for the break in her routine their visits marked, to the excitement she felt when she saw them sitting in her booth. She was past the age for romance herself and she had no illusions about her own prospects for love, but she could identify with the couple's bittersweet pleasure in seeing each other, their magnetic attraction to each other. What did they call it, vicarious pleasure?

In late April she finally decided to share her theories about the couple with Evelyn. She was sure she had figured out why the couple chose the Carolina as their meeting spot. "They're looking to meet far away enough from home that they don't run into people they know. I figure they're from near Forest City, maybe even Gastonia."

"Maybe from Spartanburg," Evelyn said. "They're safer across the state line. Plenty of motels right off the highway. His wife, or her husband, wouldn't be looking for them over here."

Gina shook her head. "If I had to guess, I'd say Pierce was a widower. Or he's been divorced."

"What makes you say that?"

"He doesn't look like he has a woman looking after him. He seems like he's a couple of weeks behind on getting his hair cut and picking up his dry-cleaning. It's Amanda who is married, probably with kids. Her husband is a dentist. Decent but dull. She's caught. She loves Pierce something fierce and is struggling over whether to leave her husband, which she doesn't want to do. She's desperate not to break up her family. But it's hard on her. Her husband just doesn't get her pilot light lit anymore, and Pierce is the best thing that ever happened to her, that ever will happen to her, and she just can't let him go."

"He's a fine looking man," said Evelyn, surprising Gina. Evelyn rarely commented on the looks of their male customers.

"That he is," Gina agreed. "He's a gentleman, too. Nice manners. And he's got some money, too, from what I can tell."

"How do you know all that?"

"I can tell. Little things. He's very courtly. He wears one of those expensive diver's watches. And he's driving a Mercedes. I haven't seen the car, but I have seen his key chain on the table."

"So is Amanda going to run off with him? He sounds too good to be true."

"I don't know," Gina said. "I haven't figured them out completely yet."

"Maybe she wants to have her cake and eat it, too. There are women like that. Plenty of them. Can't say that I like that sort at all. Talk about your selfish."

"Talk about jumping to conclusions," Gina said. "I don't think you should be passing judgment on anybody without knowing all the facts."

"If your story is half right, then what she's doing is immoral. Him, too."

"Maybe the situation is different. Maybe she's divorced and he's the married one. Maybe her ex abused her, so she left him. Their problem, their predicament, is that Pierce is married to a sick woman, one of those manic-depressives. So he's unhappily married. He once loved his wife but now she isn't quite the same person. Maybe the problem for Pierce is that if he even brings up the idea of divorce, his wife could slip over the edge and do something desperate. He's too decent and loyal a man to risk that, but Amanda ain't going to wait forever. She wants to get on with her life."

"You have an incredible imagination," Evelyn said. They had been having their conversation in the corner of the kitchen and Gina was surprised when she heard Shep clear his throat. She looked over—he had been listening intently.

"Hey, you don't have to choose just one of her explanations," he said. "All of Gina's crazy stories could be true."

"What do you mean?" Evelyn asked. "That doesn't make any sense."

"It does if there are parallel universes," Shep said. "Suppose there are other Café Carolinas and other couples in these universes. All of Gina's stories could be true. A different story for each universe."

"That's crazy," Evelyn said. "You've been watching way too much Star Trek."

"There could be other Ginas and Evelyns for that matter. Evelyn, you could even be a hot mamma in one of those universes. Sort of the exact opposite of what you are here."

"Which of the stories do you believe?" Gina asked Shep. "What's your explanation?" He turned to her, giving his full attention to the challenge.

"I couldn't rightly say," Shep said. "No question that they're stepping out, based on what I've seen. They're definitely hiding something. People get trapped, through no fault of their own. Since nobody died and made me king, I'm not the one to judge them."

"Why not judge?" Evelyn asked. "If they're cheating, it's wrong. Immoral. Plain and simple."

Shep shot her a look of disgust. "Nothing's that plain and simple," he said. "I'd guess that they're in love. It ain't just lust. If it was just about jumping into bed they'd be done by now. The only reason to keep fooling around with a married woman is when there's love. He's fallen for her in the worst way. It ain't worth the risks, otherwise. There's too much that can go wrong. Angry husbands with shotguns. Divorce lawyers. Messing up the lives of your kids, if you got 'em."

"Speaking from experience?" Evelyn asked. Shep ignored the barb.

"Somebody's gonna get hurt in this one," he said. He had a deep, husky voice, roughened by too many cigarettes, and Gina recognized a wistful tone she hadn't heard before. "They both look like they've been lonely, and loneliness can make you do crazy things."

"I don't think that it's loneliness," Evelyn said. "And that doesn't justify it."

Shep looked past her in wordless contempt. He addressed his next words solely to Gina. "You'll see what I'm talking about. Look into their eyes when you get the chance. I know it's there. You'll see it."

So she took Shep's advice and watched the couple for signs of loneliness. They seemed so wrapped up in each other that there couldn't be much room for it. She did notice that there were times when Amanda looked tired, older; the lines around her mouth seemed almost severe. That generally happened when she was by herself, but she softened when Pierce arrived with his easy smile and soft voice.

Then, on the third Monday in May, it all changed and for the worst. It was a deceptive day, colder than it looked, with rain showers off and on in the morning. Gina had shivered in her car on the way to work. Evelyn had the day off; she and her husband had gone to Spartanburg to visit his sister. Carla was covering for Evelyn and had turned up late, forcing Gina to handle most of the early crowd by herself.

They had arrived separately. Pierce turned up first, twenty minutes earlier than usual. He ordered a cup of coffee and sat in the back booth and watched the rain come down outside the Carolina through the nearby windows. When Amanda arrived, Pierce stood up and waited until she had slipped into the booth across from him before sitting back down. Gina brought her a cup of hot decaf coffee and was rewarded with an appreciative smile.

The two of them sat there for almost five minutes, drinking their coffee, without talking. Gina watched in dismay—somehow she knew something was wrong. She had never seen them so silent before. She saw Pierce reach out and gently brush his fingers over Amanda's hand; she slowly, reluctantly, withdrew her hand, avoiding his eyes. Gina noticed that she had begun twisting the wedding band on her ring finger.

Gina had to do something. She couldn't wait any longer. She went over to the booth to ask if they wanted to order any food. In the past she had waited until Pierce glanced over at her. Neither looked directly at her.

"No, thank you, ma'am," he said. "Not much of an appetite today."

Amanda responded in such a low tone of voice that Gina couldn't hear her, but she knew that she wouldn't be ordering anything either. Gina felt embarrassed at having interrupted them. She refilled their cups and wrote up their check for two coffees and left it on the table. She stood by the kitchen door, frozen in place, aware that there was nothing she could say or do that would alter what was happening. It hurt to stand there, bursting with things she wanted to say to them, but forced to remain silent—it was none of her business.

Amanda left the booth first. She had stayed only twenty minutes. She seemed unsteady on her feet. She stopped by his side of the booth and leaned into him, kissing him softly on the lips. It was the first time Gina had seen them kiss. Amanda slowly straightened up and then left the restaurant. She didn't look back.

Pierce remained at the table, his head bowed slightly. He cradled his face in his hands, his elbows on the tabletop, his eyes covered. He sat there for five minutes, not moving. Finally, he sighed, audibly, and got up awkwardly from the booth. He left money for their coffee and included a huge tip, five twenty-dollar bills. Gina knew immediately that it was the last tip he would ever leave her—it was a reward of sorts for the weeks they had occupied her booth.

She found herself moving into the aisle, blocking his way to the door, not sure why but unable to let him leave without saying something.

"Drive safely," she said, the first thing that came into her mind.

"Thank you," he said.

"See you next week, then?" she asked.

"I don't think so," he said. "But you take care."

He nodded at her and embarrassed, she moved aside, letting him pass. She knew it was over then, for sure. The next Monday there wasn't a chance that her couple would come through the Café Carolina's front door, bringing the promise of love and renewal with them. Their booth in the back would sit empty. Gina was glad that Evelyn had taken the day off to visit her sister; she wouldn't have wanted Evelyn to witness the end. Evelyn would have tried to find some moral lesson in it all, when Gina knew there wasn't any.

Eventually Gina would have to offer Evelyn some explanation for the couple's disappearance. She hoped to delay that reckoning for as long as she could. It would be a week or two before their absence became obvious. When Evelyn did ask, Gina might even lie and tell Evelyn that the couple had finally brought her into their confidence, enough to tell her that they had decided to move to California. Gina imagined the conversation that she might report to Evelyn.

"We have a few obstacles that we've overcome," Pierce would have confided to her. "Now we are free to move on. To start over." Gina would have been leaning against the side of the booth, comfortable, proud to have been trusted with the news. Pierce and Amanda would have been sitting side by side in the booth holding hands, their fingers intertwined. It would have been the first time that they hadn't faced each other, and Gina would explain to Evelyn that it signaled a new milestone in their relationship.

"It meant they were finally secure," she would tell her. "Before, when they faced each other it was almost like they were trying to memorize each other's features. Lock it into their memories. Like they might never have the chance again. When I saw them side-by-side, I said to myself that they were sure now about the future. They weren't going to be separated. There would be time enough to stare at each other as much as they liked."

"Finish with your story," Evelyn would say, eager to hear the resolution. "What happened next?"

And Gina would resume retelling Pierce and Amanda's story.

"We're going to miss this part of the country," Pierce would have explained. "Both of us grew up here. But it's best to start over. Clean slate."

"I like California," Amanda would say. "It's so warm and sunny and open. No one knows anyone there about your past. They don't care."

"Don't even bother with that," Pierce would have said to her, ignoring Gina's presence for the moment. "Let's move on. We decided, didn't we?"

"But that's important, isn't it?" Amanda would have said, never taking her eyes off Pierce. "Isn't it?"

"No," he would have said, "It isn't. We are. That's all that matters now. That's all that ever should matter."

But Gina knew that, in the end, she wouldn't lie to Evelyn. There had been no conversation. There was no future in sunny California for her couple. Pierce and Amanda would never occupy her back booth again.

She went back into the kitchen. Shep must have caught the stricken look on her face, because he asked her if something was wrong. She told him half the truth and said that she just had an upset stomach and needed some air. Gina fled to the porch overlooking the back parking lot and stood there, under the eave, avoiding the rain, hoping to regain her composure. She had a hollow, sick-to-her stomach feeling, the feeling she first had, at twelve, when they took her aside in school and told her that her mother had passed away that morning from a heart attack.

Shep poked his head out through the door. He looked at her for a long moment. "You okay, Gina?" he asked. "Everything okay?"

She nodded. Shep stepped out onto the porch to join her. He fished a pack of Kents from his back pocket, fumbling with the package to recover a cigarette. He gripped the cigarette with his one shortened finger and then lit up, blowing smoke out into the drizzle. She glanced over and saw that some of the rain had dripped from the gutter onto his bald head, beading up, but he ignored it.

"You had to know it wasn't going to last forever," he said. "A shame, in a way. But just a matter of time."

Gina didn't ask how Shep knew what had happened. Carla must have noticed and come back into the kitchen and said something to him.

"Look at it this way," he said. "How many times did we see them in here? Ten, maybe twelve Mondays? You could see how they felt something fierce for each other. Hell, I hardly saw them but once or twice and I could see it. It was all over their faces. So they had something rare, something precious, for however long it lasted. I figure that they felt more in those ten Mondays than most people do in a lifetime."

He paused to take a long drag from his cigarette. Gina found the whole situation strangely reassuring. She was amazed at the depth of Shep's observations, that he had sensed some of the same things about her couple she had. Perhaps, like Gina, he envied their passion and even their sorrow and their pain. In the time they had come into Café Carolina, into her life, she had felt more alive from just watching them.

Shep spoke again, softly, and Gina could barely hear him over the sound of the rain. "Take me. I've never had that precious thing, that fierce love. Never felt that way, or at least not when the woman felt it, too. Not even once. Not that I didn't wish for it. Hell, I prayed for it."

"Please don't say anything about this to Evelyn," Gina said. "I want to tell her."

"Sure. She ain't going to understand anyway. That woman's stone cold clueless when it comes to these matters. What would she know about heart break?"

They heard Carla calling for Shep in the kitchen, an order to place, and he turned to go back inside. "Not only did they have the love, but they must have had some killer sex." He paused, looking out past her into the back parking lot of the Carolina. "Banging like a screen door in a hurricane. I'll tell you, that's nothing to sneer at on a rainy day."

She nodded at him, afraid to say anything more for fear that she would start crying. Shep left the porch and went back into the kitchen. It had begun to rain harder, with sheets of rain sweeping across the pavement. Puddles had begun to form in the ruts along the edge of the macadam.

Gina didn't want to stay in the Carolina, she wanted to start walking, ignoring the rain, down past the Baptist church and towards the river, away from the town and the bustle of the mid-day traffic on Main Street. She could imagine her apron and uniform soaked by the rain, her hair a sodden mess, not thinking of anything but how cold and wet she had become, and how if she kept walking she wouldn't have to stay in the Carolina and see that empty last booth.

She heard Shep calling her name, softly, almost plaintively. She turned towards the door, torn, hungering to leave, to head out blindly into the rain, but knowing that Carla, hot-headed and inexperienced Carla, could never handle the Monday lunch crowd by herself.

2

Clown Prince

A postmodernist critic would have cherished Max Patkin, the Clown Prince of Baseball, as a walking, breathing, All American cultural contradiction.

Patkin spent fifty-one years entertaining at minor league ballparks around the country. In between innings, dressed in a baggy uniform with a question mark stitched on the back of his jersey instead of a number, Patkin would mug for the crowd, running through his comedy routine. He would mimic the motions of the first baseman during warm-ups. He would "teach" the third-base coach how to give signs while dancing to the song "Rock Around the Clock."

His *shtick* was baseball slapstick.

So here was the contradiction. Wasn't baseball—the great American game, our national pastime and passion—engaging enough to entertain the fans without a vaudeville novelty act? The existential question becomes, in a sense: Why Max? Why gild the lily? Why mix the profane with the sacred?

My guess is that most, if not all, of the ballplayers subjected to his comic routine hated having Max on the diamond with them. Their goal was to make it to the majors, the Bigs, and they took the game seriously. It was their job. Who needs the distraction? Who enjoys being laughed at?

Or to put it another way: Ever see a clown in a corporate board meeting? (An intentional one, that is.) Or in an operating room? Or on the floor of Congress? (I know, cheap joke).

As it happens, I met Max near the end of the his career, in the early 1990s, in a minor league ballpark in Florida. I knew the club's general manager and he introduced me to Max after the game. Max was in his early seventies and he looked it.

The Clown Prince sat on a folding chair in a cramped changing room used by the umpires. His white undershirt was drenched in sweat. I remember a gaunt, toothless man clutching a beer and complaining about the heat and the long drive he had to make the following day to the next venue. He didn't look like he was having any fun. I can't say I was surprised when I heard a few years later that he had to be hospitalized for depression.

It makes you wonder about what we find funny.

We do joke about our deepest concerns, after all. Consider, if you will, jokes about sex. For example: What's the difference between a g-spot and a golf ball? (Answer: A man will spend twenty minutes looking for a golf ball.) Or political jokes. What's the difference between Communism and capitalism? (Answer: In capitalism man exploits man and in Communism it's the other way around.) Or baseball jokes. What's the difference between a Chicago Cubs fan and a baby? (Answer: The baby will eventually stop whining.)

Freud argued that jokes had two underlying purposes—aggression and exposure. The first fueled hostile jokes and the second dirty jokes. I don't know about that. Take this joke. A man goes to his psychiatrist and asks for his help. "I keep thinking that I'm a well-known psychoanalyst," he tells him. "How long has this been going on?" the shrink asks. "Well," the man replies, "it all started when I was Jung…"

I don't think that this joke, which relies on wordplay, is hostile in the least (and it isn't dirty). So it doesn't fall into Freud's neat little categories. But wait! Maybe *telling it* is a sign of latent hostility on my part toward Freud or therapists or psychiatry. Or maybe I prefer Jungian analysis?

Those who study its nature often point to incongruity, to paradox, to surprise, and to the topsy-turvy as triggers for humor. And, more darkly, another trigger can be the misfortunes of other.

Thomas Hobbes thought laughter came from a feeling of superiority, a "sudden triumph." The *Oxford Dictionary of Philosophy* informs us that Hobbes' favorite joke involved his mother. She fell into labor with him when she heard the Spanish Armada was coming, Hobbes claimed, "so that fear and I were born twins together." Good thing Hobbes never quit his day job to try stand-up.

Brief philosophy joke: A dismayed Socrates to his friends: "I drank *what?*"

I think there's another explanation for why we want and need to laugh. After all, we live in a fallen world where people do the strangest and most awful and most wonderful things. What is it Puck says? "Lord, what fools these mortals be!" (Shakespeare joke: An actor is being booed for his lackluster performance of the famous "to be or not to be" speech in *Hamlet*. "Don't blame me," he lectures the audience. "I didn't write this shit.") Confronted with the not-so-divine comedy of everyday life, we smile because otherwise we would cry. We joke to cope.

They say Max Patkin started clowning on the baseball field in 1944. He was pitching for a Navy team in Hawaii and gave up a towering home run to Joe DiMaggio. Patkin threw his glove down and followed the Yankee Clipper around the bases, mimicking his trot.

What else can you do, Patkin was asking, when you're facing the greatest player in baseball and he demonstrates that you're not in the same league?

In fact, Patkin had a brief minor league career as a pitcher before he hurt his arm. DiMaggio's home run just confirmed that Patkin would never make it to the majors as a player.

That would be enough to make most men cry. Or laugh. And Patkin chose the latter.

3

Family Tree

The snapshot has faded, the Kodachrome leached by time and continued exposure to sunlight, the colors no longer vivid, but there we are nonetheless—Beau, Jimmy, and myself—proudly posing in front of the gigantic American beech tree that towered over the backyard of the Kincaid's house on Prospect Avenue. There we are. It's the only photograph I can find of the three of us when we were that young, an impromptu group portrait snapped by Karin Kincaid with her Brownie Starmite camera.

The last time I walked by the tree still stood there commanding the backyard. It had been pruned back somewhat by the new owners, but its branches covered most of the yard, keeping it in shade, except for the north side, where the sun catches a trellis adorned with climbing roses. The tree remains large, as large as in my memory, and that is satisfying in a world where so much seems to shrink with the passage of time.

When I look at the photo, I am struck by how handsome the boys are, squinting in the sun as they smile ("Say 'cheese'!" Karin had commanded us in her accented English). They are tall and lanky, these Kincaid boys, a family trait: Beau, thirteen years old, his dark hair long in the style of the time, on the verge of becoming a man, his intensity visible in his taut features; Jimmy, ten, still in a crew cut, with that same slightly puzzled look on his freckled face that I have always loved. You can see the men they will become in that photo, evidence of the adult persona, there, under that innocent exterior, the steel in Beau, Jimmy's endless curiosity.

And what of me? I am squeezed in between them, a head shorter, my face tilted slightly upward to the right because I had been watching Beau just before Karin clicked the shutter. I was drawn to him, always pulled by his mysterious and magnetic force. My streaked blonde hair is in bangs—I am nine years old, a year younger than Jimmy, not yet old enough to militate for the extravagant fashions of the day, the Haight-Ashbury bell bottom jeans, the psychedelic tie-dyed t-shirts in garish purples and yellows. Thank God I was too young for that grubby look. In the photo, I wear a simple jumper of light blue corduroy.

When I study the picture, I wonder about that little girl, about what I was thinking then, just before the click of the shutter. Aren't our memories like coats of paint, slapped down one on top of the other, layered and mixed together so that they cannot be separated? What I can remember are impressions from that time—still strong—of how I adored Beau, and how I believed he could do no wrong.

Beau owes his nickname to me. He had been christened Wilson and had gone by Will until I began calling him Beau, when I was eight years old, after I first saw *Beau Geste*, the movie. The name stuck, for good reason, because Jimmy and the third Kincaid brother, Desmond, followed Beau's lead just like the two younger Gestes followed their older brother in the movie. We all followed Beau.

We always climbed too high and too fast in that damn beech tree, Beau's favorite tree. But we followed his lead, all of us, and I so desperately wanted Beau to notice me, to know that I was loyal and true. So I went higher than a small, ten-year old girl should have, desperate to keep up with the Kincaid boys.

I remember the shocking suddenness of the fall, my Keds slipping on the grayish bark of the trunk and then my body weight shifting and my right hand violently tearing away from the branch. My body bounced off limbs and snapped branches on my descent, and the lush July fullness of the tree probably saved my life, painfully slowing my plunge to the ground.

It happened so quickly that all I could think was *I am falling* and then moments later I hit the ground hard, stunned by the abruptness of it all, my left arm pinned under me with a sudden sharp pain I had never experienced before.

Above me, I heard Jimmy calling for his brother, a strange, frantic note in his voice. "It was Julia. She's fallen. Hurry, you have to help her."

I knew I was hurt, but not how badly. I was scared and dazed by the fall. I stirred cautiously.

"I'm okay," I called out, struggling to catch my breath. That initial shock was starting to wear off and I could feel searing pain in my arm whenever I moved. "I'm okay," I called out, again, only I wasn't, even though I wished desperately that it was true.

It seemed only moments before Jimmy was at my side, and seconds later, Beau joined us. He had descended from the heights of the tree—like Johnny Weissmuller in one of the Tarzan movies, it seemed to me, swinging from branch to branch—and I looked up at their faces gazing down at me in concern, secretly delighted, despite the pain, by the sudden, focused attention of both older Kincaids. I sat up, cradling my left arm in my lap, and felt dizzy from the sudden surge of pain. Unbidden, tears came to my eyes.

"Where does it hurt," Beau asked.

"My arm," I told him in a whisper.

"Anywhere else?"

I bobbed my head no, but that wasn't completely the truth. I ached all over. Still, I could tell that my arm had been badly hurt. I knew tears were streaming down my cheeks, their saltiness already reaching my lips. I gritted my teeth against the throbbing pain in my arm.

"Run to the house," Beau commanded his brother. "Tell Mom that Julia fell from the tree and hurt her arm. She should call for the ambulance and for Mrs. King. Julia has to go to the hospital. I'll stay with her here."

Jimmy disappeared from sight and I heard his footsteps on the wooden steps of the Kincaid house and then the slamming of the back door.

I leaned back against the tree trunk, my left arm limp on my lap. I could see there was blood on my skin and wondered if it was from being scratched by the branches during my fall. Beau was looking intently at my arm, too, and I remembered that he had earned a Boy Scout merit badge in First Aid.

"Don't move," Beau said. "They'll be here soon and take care of you."

"It hurts," I said. "It really, really hurts."

"I'm sorry."

"It's not your fault," I told him. "I'm the one who fell."

"I should never have let you climb so high. I should have known."

"You couldn't have known, Beau," I said. "I must have slipped."

"You're very brave," Beau said to me, brushing back the bangs from my forehead and then kissing me on the cheek, gently. It was the first time that Beau—the fierce warrior when we battled with snowballs in our neighborhood wars, the leader, the architect and conductor of our play—had shown any tenderness towards me.

With his face so close to me, it was so easy for me to shift slightly and kiss him back, but full on the lips, delighting in the sensation but paying for it with a sudden jolt of burning pain in my arm. Beau heard me gasp.

"Please don't move," he said.

"I won't."

He didn't say anything about the kiss.

"I am going to stay with you," he said. "I will come to the hospital. You will be fine. They will fix your arm and it will be just fine."

In the distance I could hear the sound of an ambulance siren. It grew louder by the moment as it neared us. I believed Beau when he said I would be fine, despite the pain in my arm and my dread of what I suspected lay ahead, of the doctors and their needles. If Beau was convinced then I was convinced. I saw Beau glance over towards the house and then Jimmy and Mrs. Kincaid—the boy's ravishingly beautiful Swedish mother—appeared.

"Julia," she said. "I have telephoned and your mother is coming. How are you feeling?"

"It hurts," I said. "But it's my fault. No one else."

"It was an accident. No one is at fault."

I don't remember much more from that point on because that was when I fainted. They told me later that Beau was true to his word, staying with me as best he could. While they wouldn't let him ride in the ambulance with me (Beau had a spirited argument with the paramedic), he convinced Karin that he should go along with my mother to the emergency room.

He waited there with my mother for hours, staying through the X-rays and examinations and then my surgery.

I have a few sharply-defined memories of the hospital: the grinding sound of the X-ray machine with its evil-looking dark cone pointed at my arm; the suffocating mask descending over my face as I was anesthetized; waking up with a fresh, dazzling white plaster-of-Paris cast on my arm; and the half-surprise of finding my mother and father (who had reached the hospital then) by my bedside and my mother saying, "hello, sweetheart." I was surprised at the huskiness in my father's voice and the rush of my mother's tears.

I did not know that Dr. Brewer, the orthopedic surgeon who had set my arm, had informed my parents that the fracture had just missed the growth plate. If the break had been five millimeters closer to the wrist, he told them grimly, I might have ended up with a left arm permanently shorter than my right.

Beau wasn't allowed to see me then—even though I asked for him—but he was there when my parents brought me home the next day. Always the romantic, I hoped that his appearance might signal the beginning of love on Beau's part. Perhaps our kiss would draw him to my side. Years later I realized a more likely explanation for his behavior was simple guilt. It was *his* tree, and he hadn't kept me from falling out of it. When he came over to our house and my father brought him to the living room—where they had me propped on the couch—I insisted that he sign my cast first, and only after he had scrawled his name (*Get Well, Julia – Beau*) would I let Jimmy and Des and my other friends sign.

Beau devoted himself to my recovery, visiting every afternoon for the full three days my parents kept me inside, filling me in on the latest happenings in the neighborhood. I had a miserable summer, because the cast had to be removed, and replaced, twice and I was under strict orders not to run or engage in rough play. What was worse was that it was Beau who enforced my sentence—refusing to let me participate in anything remotely strenuous, which meant all the best games, from capture-the-flag to kickball to cannon-ball splashes in the pool, were off limits. But at least it meant Beau was paying attention to me, and I reveled in that.

When they sawed my cast off and removed the stitches I was ashamed of the atrophied wrinkled, pale arm underneath it, and the angry scar where the bone had pierced my skin. It took more than six months before my left arm looked like it belonged to me. Until then I wore unfashionable long-sleeves.

I kept the secret of my after-the-fall kiss that Beau had bestowed upon me, and the kiss on his lips I offered in response. At times I worried that in my pain and fear and confusion that I had imagined it all, but the memory was so vivid that I somehow knew it had happened. I was sure Beau remembered as well. How could he not?

I carried the secret hope that it signified something more. I believed that somehow I was destined for Beau, and he was meant for me. I just had to be patient. Beau would come to love me, I believed, and in the meantime I would stay true. I found the perfect description of the way I felt when I first read *Great Expectations* at the age of twelve. I told myself I loved Beau the way Pip loved Estella: "against reason, against promise, against peace, against hope, against happiness, against all disappointment that could be."

I guess, in the end, I was wrong. I was in college when I stumbled upon a quote from Anthony Trollope: "There is no happiness in love, except at the end of an English novel." But by then I knew that life wasn't at all like a novel. In the end, Beau wouldn't be the Kincaid brother I would marry.

That backyard photo is incomplete. It doesn't include Des Kincaid, who would have been seven years old, the third of the Kincaid brothers, nor Lisle, their little sister. Lisle is too young, just a toddler, so I'm not surprised by her absence. Des is a different matter. He was a sickly child, always battling his asthma, desperate to follow us, but often confined indoors. I can picture Des in his room, playing by himself with his cherished tin knights and a makeshift castle of wooden blocks, lost in his own private kingdom.

The tree may have been Beau's fortress, his place for testing climbing skills and courage, but for Des it became a place of refuge, his sanctuary from all that troubled him. It's not hard to explain why a child would climb a tree to get away from experiences he or she does not like—think of it, you are separated from others, free and clear from the ugliness on the ground, and you are hidden. If you climb high enough, no adult can reach you, as the tree branches will not support their weight. I think that was part of the tree's appeal for Des.

I don't pretend to know what drove Des to climb that tree more often as he grew older. I know it was common for him to ascend whenever there were arguments between Beau and his father, arguments that became more and more heated as Beau reached his late teens and asserted his independence. Professor Kincaid was not a man used to yielding, least of all to his oldest son and the war between them raged for most of Beau's high school years, with occasional truces. All of us suffered in one way or the other from that conflict.

The substance of the disputes today seem almost laughable: how long Beau could wear his hair, whether he had to continue his trumpet lessons, and what were the consequences if he broke his curfew. No doubt their arguments mirrored what was going on between fathers and their sons all over the country—perhaps all over the world.

It was almost as if a virus of rebellion had spread from teenager to teenager through the music, the clothing, the politics. In Beau's case it surfaced in different ways. It was what drove him to attend the University of Virginia against his father's expressed wishes and to enlist in the Army ROTC, of all things, which made no sense unless you understood Beau. He had a first son's self-confidence, an unshakeable faith in his own judgment.

Jimmy, the calm observer, took the conflict between his brother and father in stride. He could see both sides and he often would give me a crisp summary of the latest dispute between Beau and Professor Kincaid. It was different for Des. He shied away from confrontation. He was more likely to retreat, to escape from the situation, than deal with it directly.

One September afternoon I found Jimmy sitting on the back porch, reading a copy of *Stranger in a Strange Land*. He gave me a wan smile when he looked up.

"Beau and the Professor are at it again," he said. "Beau got him yelling, and that doesn't happen too often."

"Where's your mother?"

"She took Lisle with her to the grocery store. Beau's in his room and my father is in the study with Beethoven playing on the stereo." That meant it had been a major upheaval. Professor Kincaid saved Beethoven's Fifth for his darker moods.

"Where's Des?"

"In the tree," Jimmy said, looking over my shoulder. "Where else?"

"A bad day?"

"A bad day."

"What was the argument over?"

"What does it matter?"

I climbed gingerly up about half of the tree. I didn't want to go any higher for I remembered my fall. I had gone back and climbed it again, of course, because I didn't want anyone thinking that I was chicken. I never ventured too high, though.

Fortunately Des hadn't climbed to the top. I could see his body above me and I called out his name, but not too loudly, even though I can't imagine that we could be heard inside over the majestic strains of Beethoven emanating from the house. (When I married Jimmy I made him promise that he would never play classical music after we had quarreled. He agreed to my conditions and kept his promise. He confessed that Beethoven had been ruined for him—

he couldn't hear the music without immediately flashing on Beau and his father yelling at each other.)

Finally I had climbed high enough that Des could not pretend I wasn't there. I reached up and gently touched his sneaker resting on the juncture of the tree and the branch above me.

"What's going on, Des?" I asked.

"Not much."

"Will you come down with me?"

"I'm happy here," he said. "I don't want to be around them when they fight."

Why don't you come down and we can go for a walk?"

"Thank you, but no," he said, always the politest of the Kincaid boys. "I'll stay here."

"Are you sure?"

"I'm not like the rest of them, you know," he said suddenly, defensively.

"Who?"

"Beau and Jimmy."

"You're not?"

"I'm not as smart as them."

"That's ridiculous. Of course you are."

I didn't say out loud what I was really thinking—that I wasn't sure that I was smart enough, either, for his family's constant intellectual jousting. Could I ever hope to match wits with Beau and Jimmy, let along Professor Kincaid or Karin Kincaid? I was the daughter of a grocer and my father had attended Trenton State, barely graduating. My mother hadn't gone to college.

Des stared down at me, a challenge in his eyes.

"I'm not sure that I'm as smart as them, either," I whispered to him.

"I'll never be like them. I don't want to argue all the time and prove how smart I am. It doesn't matter, anyway, does it?"

"Why don't we go get Popsicles?" I asked. "I've got enough money for both of us."

"I like you, Julia," he said. "You're always kind to me."

"And why shouldn't I be? You're kind, too, Des. Everyone says that."

"They do?"

"Of course. Now will you come with me to the store for Popsicles?"

Des nodded reluctantly, and we both climbed down the tree. As an only child, with no brothers or sisters, I understood loneliness. I could recognize the telltale signs in Des. He was lonely. I wondered how he could feel that way, surrounded by his brothers and his sister. Of course there was more to it. Des was a loner, by nature. It was just bad luck that he had been born into the Kincaid family.

When I was a month shy of my thirteenth birthday, I persuaded my parents to let me go with the Kincaids to Florida, to Boca Grande, over the winter school break. It had been my idea and I had cleverly maneuvered Jimmy and Des into inviting me. I pointed out to my mother that I would stay with Lisle in her room, so everything would be proper, and I let the brothers convince their mother.

The Kincaids stayed in a beach house owned by Dr. Kincaid's uncle, and I did, indeed, room with Lisle, in one of the back bedrooms, but I spent much of my time with Jimmy and Des. I guess that was unusual for a girl at that age, but that's how it was.

I loved the island's narrowness—so little space between the Gasparilla Sound to the east and the Gulf of Mexico to the west—and its shady streets, with their banyan trees and ramshackle ancient cottages which had weathered a hurricane or two. I admired the turn-of-the-century look of the Port Boca Grande lighthouse at the tip of the island, next to the pass where the tarpon fishing was said to be the best in the world.

The air was sweet and warm and the sunlight seemed to cascade everywhere, illuminating everything in a clear light. The contrast to Princeton's February dingy gray couldn't have been sharper. When we waded into the Gulf, it was as warm as bath water.

I would have stayed there for months, never going back to school, if I could.

We spent the week playing tennis and swimming in the Gulf and biking around the island. Beau joined us on occasion, but he kept to himself most of the time, curling up with one of the books he always seemed to be reading (for this vacation it was Ayn Rand's *Fountainhead*).

I knew why he was moping—he was in love, and he hadn't made any headway with the girl. It made me jealous.

I acted on that jealousy one Thursday when the Professor and Karin took Jimmy, Des, and Lisle for a late lunch at the Boca Grande Club. When I found out that Beau wasn't going, I faked a headache so I could stay in the cottage.

I waited ten minutes before I brazenly invaded his bedroom and found him lying on his back, lost in thought. I sat next to him on the bed and boldly took his hand in mine. "Should I read your fortune?" I asked.

"Do you know how?" He was skeptical but he didn't pull his hand away.

I studied the palm of his hand, searching for the lifeline.

"So you really want to know your future? Who is in it?"

"That depends."

"What if I was the girl in it? In your future?"

"I'm not a cradle-robber," he said.

"I'm old enough." I held onto his hand and wriggled closer, a clumsy initial attempt at seduction. My bare leg touched his.

"I don't think so," he said. He moved away from me and rose to his feet. "I'll give you a rain check. For when you're eighteen. But by then you'll know better."

"Why wait?" I asked. I stood up and closed the distance between us. "It can be sooner than that."

Beau shook his head. "You don't really know what you are saying."

So I put my arms around his waist and pulled him to me. Before he could protest, I had kissed him on the lips hard. I pressed my small breasts firmly against his chest and he didn't break away, at first, and I sensed that he was tempted. Then he was pushing me away.

"You're too young," he said.

"No, I'm not."

My words were directed at Beau's back, because he had walked away from me, out of the bedroom, and I had to hurry to catch up to him.

I was strangely happy, for I believed that I now had acquired some sway over Beau. I had made him notice me. He would have to see me in a different light.

I was proved wrong. If anything, my advances that day opened a gap between us that never closed. Beau kept his distance from then on.

One Kincaid didn't resist me. When we became lovers—and he was my first and I was his—Jimmy told me that he thought we had always been destined to end up together. I smiled and didn't say anything. To this day I believe that we make our own destiny.

I know that I cherish that backyard photo because of how it transports me back in time, evoking all those lazy, seemingly endless days of play. The world may have in turmoil around us—Martin Luther King, Jr. and Robert Kennedy had been assassinated, murdered, in the months before the photo was snapped, American boys were dying in a war no one believed in, and in Chicago the cops were about to bludgeon the college students chanting "The Whole World is Watching"—but we played on in our leafy Princeton neighborhood, untouched by the violence and discord, oblivious to the thunderclouds and the ugliness that was descending on the country, safe in our privileged haven.

I never wanted that to end, no matter how selfish or self-absorbed that sounds today. You could argue that I got what I wanted, in some ways, connected to the Kincaids as I am. As Julia King Kincaid I became a Kincaid by marriage, although I will never completely be one to the extent that my son, Teilhard King Kincaid, is. (That's some name to give a child, isn't it? I take responsibility only for the middle name, and my son figured out very early on that he should go by "King.") Even though King is my contribution, my bit, my nine months and so much more, for continuing the Kincaid line I will always be slightly outside the circle.

Yet some would say that I am the most inside of insiders. After years of diligent study, I'm an expert about all matters Kincaid. I could be the family historian for the Princeton branch, with a specialty in modern history, say from 1965 on. Sometimes I think I know more about Beau, Jimmy, Des, and Lisle—and the Professor and Karin—than they do themselves, because I was there, fascinated, observing, taking mental notes, missing little, if anything. And I am part of that history, now, intertwined in it to the point where I have lost all objectivity, where my memories aren't completely reliable. Whose memories ever are?

4

His Madame X

He could not paint or draw or sing, but he could recognize the truly beautiful.

His keen appreciation of the aesthetic brought Kim to Manhattan, where he discovered beauty everywhere—in museums and art galleries and in the buildings and avenues of his adopted city. It was a place where he felt welcomed, and where many others cherished the beautiful.

He found a job and a fourth-floor walk-up apartment in the West Village and lived on very little but it never seemed a hardship. He was where he belonged, and he resolved never to look back over his shoulder at the small town life he had escaped. He had found beauty and freedom and he believed that love could not be far off.

During his first autumn in New York, he fell in love with Madame X. At first sight.

They met on the ground floor of the Metropolitan Museum of Art, on a quiet October afternoon when the city was bathed in warm but fading sunlight and it was hard to stay indoors.

Who wouldn't be moved? Her graceful, elongated arms, her pale skin and bare shoulders set off against a black satin dress, those jeweled straps drawing eyes to her breasts, her narrow waist and the curve of her hips. Her profile was arresting, sensual. Some might find her nose too pronounced, but Kim found it appealing.

After he saw her, he was driven to learn about her creator, John Singer Sargent. He haunted the New York Public Library in his spare time, researching Madame X—Virginie Amélie Avegno Gautreau—who, like Sargent, had lived as an American expat in Paris. Not surprisingly, men were magnetically attracted to her. Rumors circulated of infidelities. It was said that she paid little attention to the boundaries of marriage. She was a woman who cared little for convention.

Kim was thrilled when he discovered that John Singer Sargent, a lifelong bachelor, had painted hundreds of canvases of men posing in the nude. "Just like da Vinci and Michelangelo," his friend Diego commented. "Forced into the closet." Kim purchased a copy of *John Singer Sargent: The Male Nudes* at the Strand Bookstore and poured over the color plates, delighted to find traces of the same beauty he had encountered with Madame Gautreau.

He still preferred the *Portrait of Madame X* and wasn't surprised to learn that Sargent considered it his best work. Yet the painting had been trouble for the artist from the start. Sargent knew the aesthetic effect that he wanted—he especially loved his subject's wonderful lines—but he struggled with almost aspect of the painting.

Madame Gautreau reluctantly agreed to sit for him. She didn't like the pose he chose for her, standing with her face in profile. The bluish color of her skin in clear light proved a major difficulty and Sargent experimented until he finally found a mix of light rose and green that seemed a better choice to represent her skin tone. He labored over the look of her right arm, repainting it numerous times. In the end, his original canvas was so thickly coated with paint that he decided to copy the image onto a fresh canvas.

Sargent's masterpiece didn't get the reception he had hoped for when it was shown at the Palais des Champs-Elysées as part of the Salon of 1884. The Parisians who attended the first day mocked and reviled the portrait. Madame Gautreau's mother showed up at his studio to demand that he remove the painting from the Salon—claiming that it was ruining her daughter's reputation. Sargent refused to withdraw it.

The hostile reception hurt his standing as an artist. A Sargent portrait no longer was a fashionable expenditure for the bourgeoisie. To make a living, Sargent was forced to relocate to London. Only years later did the critics and the public appreciate the artistic virtues of *Portrait of Madame X*.

But Sargent never wavered in the belief that he had captured the essence of Madame Gautreau. He hung the painting in his London studio. When he sold it to the Metropolitan Museum of Art in 1916, he told the director that it was the best thing he had ever done.

Kim had many affairs during his first years in the city. When it appeared that it might become something more than a one-night stand, he devised a simple test designed to surface the true nature of his would-be boyfriend. He would bring his new lover to the Met and they would stroll through the galleries until they reached *Portrait of Madame X*. Kim would make sure that they paused before the painting, but he would remain silent. He would wait to see the reaction of his lover.

Some said nothing. Others would comment about the portrait—at times with surprising knowledge of artistic technique—but yet miss the sublime nature of Sargent's painting, the subtle and unspoken. It was frustrating that he didn't find anyone who could see what he saw. But he kept trying.

Kim came out to his parents after his second year in the city. He told them when he returned home at Christmas. He waited until early in the morning he was due to fly back to New York, figuring that he could always use the excuse that he had to get to the airport in Pittsburgh if things got too heavy. He knew it might hurt his parents, who loyally occupied the third pew at the Central Presbyterian Church every Sunday, but he also felt a need to affirm who he really was.

His father received the news impassively. He was never one for displays of emotion. Kim's mother burst into tears and confessed that she had always known her son was different. Kim suppressed the urge to say "No kidding." Then she hugged him.

He spent the flight back staring out the window at the landscape below. He took a cab from LaGuardia direct to the Met and arrived only forty-five minutes before closing. He hurried to the gallery with *Portrait of Madame X* and stayed there, savoring the brushwork and the colors and her proud acceptance of who she was, until the guard gently reminded Kim that it was time to go.

5

Something More Than This

In the morning, the front desk clerk warned John Lee to be careful. "You might want to avoid the Old City for now," he told him. The clerk, a smallish man with wire-rimmed glasses and slicked-back dark hair, had a clipped, vaguely British accent. "There was a terrorist incident at the Damascus Gate yesterday. A woman was killed."

The man handed John Lee a copy of the *Jerusalem Post*. The front page told of the stabbing death of a West German tourist, just inside the Damascus Gate, the entrance to the Arab Quarter of the Old City.

"Thanks for the warning," John Lee said, after briefly scanning the article. "Judging from the story, the attack came out of nowhere. Almost at random."

From behind the counter, the clerk surveyed him with sad eyes. "No, not at random," he said. "I wouldn't call it random. It was deliberate. They target European and American tourists. To discourage you from visiting."

"Has it worked?"

"Yes. It has hurt tourism. But as nasty as these incidents are, the bombs are worse. They kill many, many people. Indiscriminately."

John Lee returned the newspaper to him without comment. Then he handed the clerk his room key, for safekeeping, and a letter he had written to Maureen on the flight over, filled with some of the things he had wanted to say to her but hadn't. "Could you please mail this for me?" he asked.

"Certainly," the clerk said. He paused for a moment. "You could perhaps visit Yad Vashem, the Holocaust museum, today. Or go shopping downtown. You could wait until later in the week to visit the Old City. Things should be calmer then."

John Lee thanked him for the suggestions. He didn't tell the clerk that he planned to ignore his advice and visit the Old City that day, anyway, despite the stabbing. Changing his itinerary went against John Lee's nature. He had planned three days in Jerusalem, and he didn't want to waste any of his limited time there.

There was another reason to stick to his schedule. John Lee had been taught that only God decided when, where, and how He would call his children home. Even though he had lost his faith in the omnipotent Southern Baptist God of his childhood, he hadn't completely abandoned that deterministic worldview. Now he would call it fate, but he still respected the notion that some things were out of human control.

He wouldn't run scared. The odds were more likely that he would be nailed crossing the street by one of the city's reckless drivers than confront a terrorist attack. But he would be more cautious. It was clear that the *intifada*, the Palestinian uprising against Israeli rule on the West Bank, was for real.

A month earlier the travel agent in Tallahassee had tried to talk him into an elaborate "Pilgrim's Package," but John Lee finally persuaded her that all he needed were hotel reservations in Jerusalem and Tiberias and a car rental. He was too independent for a tour. He didn't want to be tied to an itinerary not of his own choosing. He asked her to find moderately priced hotels near the center of town. (John Senior would have approved of his traveling on the economy plan.)

Memories of his father had dominated his thoughts the night before, when John Lee had arrived. On the long silent cab ride from Lod airport he wondered why, when his father was still alive, John Senior had never said anything about wanting John Lee to visit Jerusalem and the Galilee. Presumably he feared his son's rejection of the idea.

It was true, in the narrowest sense, that John Lee did not have to make the trip. He could have told Harry Newberry, his family's long-time attorney and executor of his father's will, that he couldn't accept the terms of the bequest, in which case the money would have gone to charity, to Baptist missionary work in the Middle East. That was what Maureen had suggested.

When he asked her if she wanted to come along to Israel, she had shrugged. "This is your thing," she said. "I would be in the way."

"No, you wouldn't."

"I would," she said. "Or I'd feel that I was, or I'd feel really weird. This whole trip, the idea itself, is more than a little strange, but I guess you know that already. It's Meredith strange." That was Maureen's label for any behavior by John Lee's family that she considered weird, such as John Lee calling his parents by their first names.

"You obviously feel you have to go," she said.

"I do," he said. "I don't see I have a choice."

"That's in your head. There is always a choice. You don't have to do what you don't want to."

He just shook his head. "It's the least that I can do."

Maureen didn't understand that by making it one of his last requests John Senior had made it impossible for John Lee to decline.

"Don't worry," she said with a mischievous grin when it became clear that he was going. "I'll be here when you get back. Unless I get a better offer."

Harry Newberry had given him his father's Bible, the leather cover creased and worn, after they read the will together. A month before he died, John Senior had insisted Newberry take the Bible for safekeeping.

When John Lee was a boy, his father had read the Bible to him almost every night at bedtime. John Lee would pull the covers of his comforter to his chin and listen to the rumble of his father's voice, secretly repelled by much of what he heard, the angry Jehovah of the Old Testament, the God who turned Lot's wife into salt, tormented Job with afflictions, who seemed to throw temper tantrums whenever the Israelites disobeyed Him.

John Lee never told John Senior that, of course. Instead, he asked him to read passages from the Gospel according to John, or from the mystical poetry of the Psalms. He did not doubt that his father had guessed the reasons for his request, but John Senior never asked him why.

The night of his arrival, as the cab hurtled along the highway and he caught glimpses of Jerusalem's lights on the highlands above, John Lee wondered when it was his father had inserted the language about the trip into his will; after Emma's death, probably, which meant it would have been in the past three years. John Senior's motives seemed transparent: the hope that John Lee's pilgrimage would somehow revive his faith, that physical proximity to the holy sites would miraculously rekindle the belief that his son had abandoned in college. But John Lee knew that wasn't going to happen. He would visit the historical sites and play tourist for ten days. That would discharge his obligation.

At the same time John Lee suspected that his father found some humor in the idea of John Lee, the skeptic, the doubting Thomas, making the pilgrimage to Israel. His father had always appreciated the odd and absurd, the contradictions in life.

He fought back a sudden wave of nausea as the cab reached the outskirts of the city; it was a sign of anxiety and nervousness he had experienced before. His watch read ten o'clock when John Lee finally arrived at the quiet West Jerusalem side-street where his hotel was located. He paid the cab driver and checked in at the front desk, anxious to retreat to the privacy of his room. He followed the porter (by his looks a Palestinian) to a cramped and shabby elevator, where they rode in silence to the third floor. Once in his narrow room, John Lee lay down on the single bed and took a few deep breaths, fighting back his nerves. He tried clearing his mind and thinking of the other times he had been in strange and unfamiliar places and how he had lost his anxiety and enjoyed himself.

There was no television in the room, just a battered clock radio on the night table near a floor lamp. John Lee switched on the radio and heard a deep-voiced announcer speaking in Hebrew. He ducked into the undersized bathroom where he washed his hands and face with the hotel's thin bar of soap, drying himself with the faded, lightweight towel. A familiar song by an English band whose name he couldn't remember came on the radio; the chorus—something about "right here, right now, watching the world wake up from history"—seemed somehow fitting.

His nausea had subsided by then, replaced by the beginnings of a dull headache. The music on the radio made him wish he had brought his guitar, which was a fail-safe comfort in anxious times. He always found comfort in fingering chords or composing a melody. But he had decided to travel light, and so he had left his guitar and its bulky case behind in Tallahassee.

He tried reading his Fodor's guidebook, but the light from the floor lamp bothered his eyes. So he took two aspirin and went to bed, hoping to sleep off the effects of the long flight from Miami. He heard the sounds of the elevator and of people moving up and down the corridor and then he fell asleep.

In the morning, after he had left the hotel, John Lee wandered around downtown for a few hours. His plan was to stop at locations he'd culled from the travel guides he'd read before the trip. He had carefully marked the spots on his map. Buddy, his latest drummer, had kidded John Lee about his preparation. "You're too damn serious about this," Buddy said. "It ain't like you're going to be tested on what you've seen when you get back."

"No, I'm not," John Lee conceded. "But I like to know where I am."

"Suit yourself," Buddy said. "Me, I like to be spontaneous. To go with the flow."

His father had first taught his son how to read a map when John Lee was twelve and they had gone camping together in northwest Texas, near the New Mexico border. His father had John Lee plot their route to the next campsite using a U.S. Geological Survey map and John Senior's German-made compass. John Senior had praised the certainty of maps to his son.

"With a map and a compass you're never lost," he explained.

"But you have to know where you are," John Lee objected. "You need a point of reference."

"Put me anywhere in the world with a half-decent map, and I'll find some landmarks and then I'll plot a way back home. There are always going to be landmarks, John."

With his father's battered compass in his front trouser pocket for luck, John Lee strolled through Independence Park, past the Town Hall, built after the Israelis' victory in the Six Day War, and then skirted the massive Russian

Cathedral with its green cupolas. He took a slight detour into the Russian Quarter before turning back to the west.

The downtown had a cosmopolitan, European feel to it, with its broad boulevards and limestone-faced buildings. Most of the young people he saw on the street were dressed casually in jeans and t-shirts like their American counterparts, and John Lee noticed at several intersections, mini-billboards promoting Kevin Costner in the movie *Robin Hood*. That part of the street scene seemed familiar to him, but the ever-present Israeli soldiers, many of them just kids themselves, and the groups of black-clad Orthodox men striding along the sidewalks, did not.

John Lee walked back through the Merkaz Mis'hari section, using the domed tower of the YMCA building as a reference point, until he reached the Yemin Moshe Quarter, near the Montefiore Windmill. He had an appointment for lunch at a nearby restaurant, at noon, with Lucas Spring, a Baptist minister who had been a college friend of his father.

Spring had lived in Jerusalem for ten years and made his living by guiding Baptist groups on tours of Israel. When John Lee found that his father had paper-clipped Spring's business card to the will, he figured that he was meant to call him. They'd agreed to meet for lunch on John Lee's first day in Jerusalem, the only time Spring was available.

John Lee found the Windmill Restaurant on a crooked side street within sight of the southwestern wall of the Old City. He arrived a few minutes before noon and found the place nearly empty except for a few bored waiters and Spring, who was waiting for him in the bar at the front of the restaurant. Spring quickly explained that he'd only been there for five minutes, as if, absent his explanation, John Lee would assume he'd become a West Jerusalem barfly.

Spring was a large, fleshy man with silver hair and a deep voice, a voice John Lee could easily imagine soaring and falling in the roller-coaster cadences of a Sunday sermon. John Lee guessed that the man was in his late sixties; he remembered that Spring had been a contemporary of his father at the seminary in Houston.

Once they had been seated at a table, Spring began with another apology that he wouldn't be able to offer John Lee a personal tour of Jerusalem and the Galilee. "Like I told you on the phone, I'm retiring in a few weeks," he said. "To the other land of milk and honey, back to the United States. I stopped guiding tours last week to give me some time to pack up for the move. There are a million loose ends to tie up."

"Where are you planning to settle?" John Lee asked.

"I'm not sure yet," Spring said, without glancing up from his menu. He had a pair of dark-rimmed half glasses perched on the bridge of his nose. "I'll stay with my sister in Raleigh for a time and then decide."

A waiter arrived at their table and Spring ordered a tabbouleh salad and couscous with chicken. John Lee asked for the only dish on the menu he recognized, hummus with lamb. Spring assured him that it was a specialty of the restaurant.

"You do look like your father," Spring said. "Especially around the eyes. I can see the resemblance." He paused. "I'm sorry for your loss. I never spent a great deal of time with him, but I respected and admired your father."

"Thank you," John Lee said, hoping that Spring wouldn't dwell on John Senior's death. He hoped to avoid any religious pep talk about how his father was better off now that he had joined the rest of the Saints on the Other Side.

"I never did get around to asking your father whether you're related to Don Meredith," Spring began. "Your family's been in Texas forever, hasn't it?"

"Dad was from Austin, and Don Meredith's from Mount Vernon, in Franklin County. We may be distant relations, but I couldn't claim him as kin."

Spring seemed disappointed in the answer. "I haven't been able to follow the Cowboys here," he said. "Let alone Baylor. The *Trib*'s football coverage is spotty. Fortunately they show the Super Bowl on TV here, otherwise I'd miss that as well."

"We're about a third of the way through the season," John Lee said. "The Cowboys are off to a good start. You'll get all the football you could want once you get back home."

"I'm looking forward to that," Spring said. "That and Christmas. You'd have to live here to understand how little attention is paid to Christmas. Makes all of us expats homesick. At the same time, a part of me wishes I could stay. I will miss this city. And the Sea of Galilee. That's an amazing place."

"It's on my list to visit."

"I tell you what I won't miss," Spring said, shifting in his chair. "Since the *intifada* began everyone seems to be waiting for something really horrific to happen. It wasn't like that when I first came here. There was more of a live and let live attitude. That's gone."

"Has there been a lot of violence?" John Lee asked.

"Sporadic," he said. "Like the stabbing yesterday. The police and the army will be all over the Old City for the next week or so. Today at least the Old City should be safe. Another one of those paradoxes about this place."

"What's the solution?" John Lee asked. "Make Jerusalem an international city?"

"Neither side would accept that," Spring said. "It's too logical, too American. I gave up trying to figure out a solution a while back. It's a waste of time even considering the political situation, so I don't."

Spring shrugged in resignation. "So there you have it." He took off his half-glasses and retrieved a case from his sports coat to put them in. He turned his attention back to John Lee. "So what brings you to Jerusalem?" he asked. "I've learned over the years that most everyone who comes here has a very personal reason."

"It's my father," John Lee found himself explaining. "It was in his will, a legacy of sorts. He set aside some money for me to visit Jerusalem and the Galilee. The only stipulation was that I had to take the trip within a year of his passing."

"That's a marvelous idea," Spring said. "If Amy and I had been blessed with children, I'd have made sure that they spent time here."

John Lee remembered that Spring was a widower. He had learned from Harry Newberry that Spring moved to Israel shortly after his wife's death. "Maybe he thought he could leave his grief behind," Newberry said. "That never works, though, does it? I know at the time the move struck me as odd but your father seemed to understand it. Considering how he reacted to Emma's passing, it makes some sense."

Almost as if he had guessed what John Lee was thinking, Spring began explaining his reasons for coming to Jerusalem. "I'd always been intrigued when I had visited over the years," he said. "When Amy died I was at a loss as to what to do. Then I opened my Bible and came upon Psalm One hundred and twenty two. I felt like it was written for me, all those wonderful verses about going to the house of the Lord and standing within the gates of Jerusalem. I saw it as a sign. I'm confident it was. I put my affairs in order and bought a plane ticket here. That was almost ten years ago."

"It's a long way from Dallas."

"You know what T.S. Eliot said about pilgrimage sites?" Spring asked. He didn't wait for John Lee to answer. "They are places where prayer had been valid. That's true for here, you know. Prayer has been valid here for centuries. Dallas has a ways to go to catch up."

John Lee nodded. "My Dad was taken with this place, too. He had been here once, on a pilgrimage of sorts, and talked about the impression it made on him. He always wanted to come back. I guess he wanted me to have the same experience."

"So are you using up vacation time?" Spring asked.

"I'm self-employed, I guess you could say," John Lee said. "So I vacation whenever it doesn't interfere with touring. I've got my own band, country-rock. There are five of us and we play mainly around Tallahassee. We'll jump over to Pensacola or down to Tampa and Gainesville now and then, but our base is Tallahassee."

"What is your role in the band?" Spring asked.

"I play lead guitar and sing. All those years in the choir. I've put them to good use."

"You enjoy it," Spring said. "I can tell.

"It is what I want to do. For now."

"You're young. You should be trying things out."

"I can tell you that my father wasn't crazy about my singing. I'm afraid it was a bit of a disappointment."

Spring made no reply. That John Senior had been disappointed with John Lee's choice of careers went without saying. His father had not considered it serious work. But John Lee didn't want his life to be shaped by the expectations of others, especially those of his father.

The waiter returned to clear their table of the lunch dishes. Spring had a cup of black Turkish coffee and John Lee ordered a Coke. Spring talked about a fishing trip he hoped to take with his brother-in-law in Florida. They were planning to go offshore for marlin. John Lee listened politely.

When they had finished their drinks, Spring insisted on paying for lunch. They paused at the front door of the restaurant, Spring resting his hand lightly on John Lee's arm, keeping him there for a moment. Spring squinted in the light, wincing from its harshness after the dark of the restaurant. In the natural light, John Lee saw that Spring had the pallor of a sick man. He wondered whether Spring's departure had been prompted by poor health.

"We don't always get around to saying the things we need to say," Spring said. "After Amy was gone I thought of a million things I wanted to say to her that I never did." He looked at John Lee and smiled. "If your father was here today, I'm sure he'd tell you that you were never a disappointment to him. Some of your choices may have disappointed him, but not you."

"Thanks," said John Lee, embarrassed by Spring's comments. He promised to look up the older man if he ever found himself in Raleigh. They shook hands awkwardly, and Spring slowly walked away, back toward the center of the city.

John Lee briefly consulted his map and found an alleyway that brought him to Hativat Street. From there, with the masonry walls of the Old City and a massive construction site before him, he made his way east, following the tour buses and taxis headed in that direction.

As he moved through the Jaffa Gate he felt the muscles in his shoulders tighten slightly. It was absurd, he knew, but he couldn't help himself. It seemed that there were Israeli soldiers with ugly-looking snub-nosed weapons everywhere. To his right, the dark walls of the ancient Citadel blocked his view as he moved into the open space of the plaza.

He bumped into an elderly woman, almost knocking her down. He began to apologize but stopped when she raised her hands in the air and fixed her pale blue eyes on him. She was an odd looking figure, with leathery skin, a shock of white hair tucked under a khaki bush hat, and one front tooth slightly askew. He guessed that she had to be at least seventy years old.

"Don't apologize," she said. "It's my fault. I didn't move fast enough and get out of your way."

John Lee guided the old woman out of the stream of foot traffic to a nearby alcove. She leaned on his arm, her fingers gripping the fabric of his shirt.

"I'm Australian," she told him. "An Aussie. But you can tell that, I'll bet. A pilgrim from Geelong. That's southwest of Melbourne, although I'll bet Geelong could be Woop Woop as far as you're concerned."

"I'll confess that I've never heard of Geelong before," John Lee told her. "Or Woop Woop." He introduced himself and the woman shook his hand.

"My name is Connie Wilcox," she said. "But you can call me Con. That's what they call me back home. Where are you headed? You're a pilgrim, too, I take it."

"To the Western Wall, first. Then some of the other sites in the Old City."

"That's a fine start," she said. "I'll tag along, if you don't mind." She lowered her voice and peered over her shoulder, ready to share a secret. "I didn't care for the schedule the church group was following, so I made my escape. I'm glad God saw fit to send you along. The Wall is my first stop on the tour today. I remember it well from my last trip. Need help, though. My arthritis is kicking up."

"You weren't put off by the incident at the Damascus Gate yesterday?"

She fixed her gaze on him again, scrutinizing him with a fierceness he found both disconcerting and strangely reassuring. "The stabbing? Wouldn't delay my pilgrimage two seconds because of that. Can't afford to wait. These people have been quarreling with each other for thousands of years. The church group took a fright and decided to go to Bethlehem today. I don't understand that at all. God takes care of his children." She paused. "How old do you think I am?"

John Lee shook his head, declining to guess.

"I'm seventy-seven," she said. "With a full hip replacement and arthritis. That won't stop me. It won't slow me down either. Not when I travel with the Holy Spirit."

It was clear to him now that Connie Wilcox wasn't completely balanced; whether she was clinically disturbed was a question he couldn't begin to answer. John Lee had never been comfortable around the emotionally fragile; his mother always had an affinity for them—she knew how to treat the disturbed and the troubled with a gentle matter-of-factness, always steering them back closer to reality.

They turned southward following the Street of the Armenian Patriarchate, which would eventually take them to the outside of the Jewish Quarter and the Western Wall. As they slowly made their way, she told John Lee rambling, disjointed stories of her three prior visits to Jerusalem, and of her life in Geelong. He listened patiently.

"I've been yabbering a bit here," she said. "It's my enthusiasm. I love coming back here. It's like a second home for me, to walk where Jesus walked, to pray at these holy places."

They had to move slowly. John Lee could hear her breathing heavily, wheezing, whenever he hastened their pace. But she limped alongside him without complaint. He fought back his irritation at their slow progress.

After about ten more minutes, John Lee could see that she needed to rest. He persuaded her to stop briefly at a small cafe that had a few worn tables and chairs outside. She carefully lowered herself onto one of the chairs. They ordered Coca Colas and the owner, a small, elderly Arab with a wispy mustache, brought them glass bottles beaded with condensation. Connie drank her soda quickly, sucking loudly on the straw. John Lee had to admire her toughness. She had to be descended from one the convicts the English had exiled to Australia to populate their distant imperial outpost.

"My father was a minister," he told her. "Southern Baptist. He's the only reason I'm here today."

"He would be very proud of you," she said. "To see you here, and to know that he raised you up in the way of the Lord."

"You're not following me. My father paid for this trip. He always wanted me to see Jerusalem. I would never have come if he hadn't left me the money in his will."

"What's wrong with that?" she asked. "You make it sound like there's something wrong with that."

"No, there's nothing wrong," he said, realizing that he wouldn't be able to have a normal conversation with her. He regretted that he hadn't rebuffed her at the Jaffa Gate.

"You think I'm not all here, don't you?" she asked him, fixing her gaze on him. "You think I'm a bit daft, don't you?"

"Why do you think that?"

"I'm not," she said. "I'm not daft. Just a bit scattered. You'll find that happens when you get older. Wait and see, my boy." Satisfied that she had set the record straight, she returned to sipping her drink.

She insisted that they press on to the Temple Mount. He checked his watch quickly; glad to be on the move again. John Lee was impatient to reach the Wall, and he didn't want to devote too much of his afternoon to getting there. He thought of Maureen for a moment. He should have insisted that she join him on the trip—the day would have been completely different. They wouldn't have been sidetracked by Connie Wilcox; Maureen would have politely discouraged her from the start.

John Lee negotiated their way along the street ringing the outside of the Armenian Quarter. The masonry wall to their right, separating them from the traffic of the New City, provided a sense of security and isolation. On the map, John Lee saw that they could skirt most of the Jewish Quarter by staying with their current route, arriving at the Wall without having to traverse too many side streets.

He wasn't disappointed by the scene when they did reach the Western Wall. John Lee had studied the guidebook's photographs, but he was still impressed by the broad sweep of the square, the white-and-blue Star of David flags flapping in the breeze, the solidity and scale of the Wall with its huge, square-hewn limestone blocks and the glittering golden Dome above. The Wall itself seemed higher than the sixty feet the guidebook estimated. Some of the ashlar blocks had to be at least thirty feet long.

The open space directly in front of the Wall was crowded with clusters of people, many swaying, bobbing, and nodding in prayer. At one end the black-clad observant had gathered where a barrier separated men from women. Many had their hands and faces pressed against the huge stones. Skinny Israeli soldiers in combat fatigues and berets patrolled the plaza.

John Lee found it amazing that thousands of pilgrims of all faiths would trek there, to the same geographic spot, as if those worn stones and ancient buildings at that specific latitude and longitude were somehow closer to heaven than wherever they lived. It had to be a heresy, he thought, that God could be found in a more concentrated form in Jerusalem than in Tallahassee, Florida or Geelong, Australia.

He wondered whether that reflected the essential absurdity of tourism, traveling great distances to gawk at someone else's broken-down buildings and hear sad and fabulous tales of the past while, at the same time, the exact same journey was being made in the opposite direction, as foreigners, fellow tourists, visited your country's historical sites. Emma had maintained that yard sales worked in the same way. You sold your junk to your neighbors at your yard sale, and then bought their castoffs when they held their own. It was recycling at its best, she claimed, because the total amount of junk remained constant.

Connie interrupted his reverie with an abrupt tug on his right hand. She kept his hand firmly in her grip and began loudly praying. "Jesus, we are here," she said, "Jesus, we praise and glorify you." Then she began praying so quickly that the words ran together: "Jesus-we-praise-you-Son-of-God." A moment later she began speaking in tongues—words and sounds pouring out of her in an incomprehensible stream.

He looked around, embarrassed, but found that the other visitors to the Wall were ignoring Connie. He realized that her fervor wasn't out of place in the slightest—it was his own emotional and spiritual distance that was strange, foreign.

John Lee had witnessed tongue speaking once before, in Texas, when he had attended a Pentecostal service with his father. John Lee had just turned twenty, back from college over a Christmas holiday, and he had tried to provoke an argument with John Senior over whether tongue speaking represented a gift of the Holy Spirit or group-induced hysteria.

His father had been patient with him. He spoke calmly, although John Lee noticed that his face seemed more flushed than usual.

"I won't debate this with you," he said. "What you think or I think about their speaking in tongues doesn't matter. Or what you may have learned in an introductory psychology course. What matters is what happens in the hearts of the people in that church. How they live out the Gospel."

"The truth doesn't matter?" John Lee had asked sharply, stung by his father's gentle rebuke.

"Whose truth? You'll find the truth that you're looking for. If you want to shut yourself off from the Holy Spirit, you will. These people haven't."

"How can you be so sure?"

"I can only be sure for myself," he said, and then with great tenderness, "I would give anything for you, John, to share that conviction."

"I'm sorry," John Lee said. "But I don't share it."

John Lee found himself blinking back tears at the memory. He had never been able to offer his father that gift of certainty, no matter how much he had wished at times that he could.

Connie had stopped speaking in tongues. She had her arms lifted to the sky, and her eyes closed. She stood, motionless, for a minute or two and then she slowly opened her eyes and looked over at John Lee.

"Maybe later," she said. "Maybe the Holy Spirit will touch you later."

"Maybe," he said. "I'm moving nearer to the Wall."

He noticed a few pigeons perched on clumps of caper bushes wedged between the large, pale stones, higher up on the Wall. In some spots, there were weeds growing as well. He found himself drawn even closer. There was something elemental, yet magical, about the Wall's simplicity. It was just there, he thought, acting as a mirror of the emotions of the people facing it, bouncing back whatever feelings were inside.

"I'm here," he said quietly. He reached out and touched the stone in front of him. He liked its feel, still warm from the midday sun, on his finger tips. He thought of John Senior and Emma, and he struggled to hold back the emotion. "I'm here," he whispered, this time to his parents, even though he knew it was a foolish gesture.

He felt a tugging at his elbow. It was Connie. She had been watching him, he realized, and he felt a flash of irritation. Couldn't she leave him alone, even for a few moments? He had tired of her company.

"I'm right here," she said. "Are you ready to shoot through to our next stop? I could use a hand to get to the Church of the Holy Sepulchre. We can break our trek on the way for another cool drink if you like, or we can push on now and steal a march on the tourists."

"The Church of the Sepulchre?" He couldn't help but turn back and gaze up at the Temple Mount. Connie Wilcox saw where he had glanced.

"I don't think I have the energy for climbing up there and touring the place," she said. "To be truthful, I'm also not sure we're that welcome today."

He remained silent, again annoyed. They had been much closer to the Church of the Holy Sepulchre when they had first met near the Jaffa Gate. She should have told him then, so that they could have visited the church first before making the longer walk to the Wall.

He thought about inventing an excuse and leaving Connie Wilcox to fend for herself. He hadn't asked to be trapped by her side, the victim of a chance encounter. He glanced at his watch, checking the time, and then flushed, embarrassed, when he realized Connie Wilcox had seen the gesture.

She looked at him, unperturbed, and then asked him directly whether it would be too much of a bother to stay with her, almost as if she had been reading his mind. "I imagine I can find someone else to help," she said, "if you can't."

"Of course I can," John Lee said quickly, responding to the plaintive tone in her voice. He thought again of John Senior and his hopes for this trip and knew then, with certainty, that he would stay with Connie Wilcox until she needed him no longer. There wasn't a real choice involved.

She brightened at her easy victory, a smile creasing her face.

"Let's pray," she said. "Join me this time, John Lee, won't you? There's something about praying together that's inspiring."

He knew she wouldn't rest until he had relented and prayed with her. He resigned himself to going through the motions. She knelt on the stone of the plaza floor and he followed suit, wincing when a loose pebble pressed into his knee. She closed her eyes and spread her arms and began praying in a loud, hoarse voice.

John Lee closed his eyes. He tried to tune out her voice, thankful when she again began speaking in tongues. It was less distracting than her intelligible prayers. He found himself relaxing, enjoying the warmth of the afternoon sun and the light breeze from the east. He thought about how he would convey the absurdity of the scene to Maureen, and realized he only had to describe it and she would crack up at the idea of John Lee as Jesus Freak, brought to his knees in the Jerusalem's Old City.

"There you are, John Lee," he heard a deep voice say and, startled, he opened his eyes. He found Lucas Spring looming over him, a pleased look on his face. Spring's shirt was soaked in perspiration and he was breathing heavily. His sports coat was loosely draped over one arm. John Lee scrambled to his feet, brushing the dust off his knees of his pants, embarrassed at the situation. Spring seemed excited about something.

"This is great," Spring said. "I didn't expect I'd be able to find you. I figured you might have reached the Wall by now, but it was a long shot. If you were up there," he said, jabbing a finger at the Temple Mount, "I never would have found you."

"It took longer to get here than I had planned," John Lee said. "A few complications along the way."

"I only arrived here myself maybe five minutes ago," Spring said. "I got lucky and spotted you in the crowd. Your maroon baseball cap stood out a mile away. Florida State's colors, right?"

John Lee nodded. There was an awkward silence. He noticed that Connie Wilcox had stopped praying out loud. He was sure that she was listening intently to their conversation.

"You must be wondering why I'm here," Spring said. "It's simple, actually. After our lunch, I walked half of the way back to my apartment before I decided to come find you. I felt a need to be here. Skipping an afternoon of packing won't matter much, one way or the other. I can finish off the Old City for you, give you the nickel tour. That's the hospitable thing to do."

Spring stopped, distracted by Connie Wilcox's sudden appearance. She had moved to the right of John Lee, where the top of her head barely reached the level of his shoulder. She looked up, peering at them, her eyes moving from one man to the other, studying their faces. John Lee knew that she was expecting an introduction to Spring, but he waited for her to speak first.

"John Lee," she said. "Are you going to introduce me to your friend?"

"Lucas Spring," John Lee said. "This is Connie Wilcox. We met back at the Jaffa Gate."

"A pilgrim," she said, gripping Spring's free hand with both of hers. "A pilgrim who has been escorted this fine Tuesday by this wonderful young man. He's been a help and a comfort throughout the day. Praise the Lord."

Spring glanced over for guidance, but John Lee just shrugged in response.

"From what I know of John Lee," Spring said, "I'm not surprised."

"To tell the truth he reminds me of my own son," she said. "Both of them very tall. Except I lost Alastair early. The Lord took him early."

"I'm sorry," Spring said. She bobbed her head in reply.

"How long have you known John Lee?" she asked Spring, who had gently disengaged his hand from hers.

"We just met today. But I was friendly with John Lee's father back in Texas. A wonderful man. We went to school together in the old days."

"Hah," she said. "I know those old days, those good old days."

"Reverend Spring gives tours of the Holy Land," John Lee explained.

"He gives tours, does he?" she asked, her tone playful. "I've just escaped from a tour. I didn't want to be stuck with that group. They didn't have the faith to risk a visit to the Old City. I do. Nevertheless, I shouldn't be completely on my own because I'm not as spry as I once was. That's why John Lee has been such a God send, although I'm not sure he sees it that way. It's not easy putting up with an ancient like myself."

"You've kept me on my toes," said John Lee. "It's been an adventure."

"I'm glad you turned up, Reverend Spring," said Connie, focusing her attention on him. "You can show us the fastest route to the Church of the Holy Sepulchre. And fill us in on the marvelous history along the way."

Spring nodded. "I'd be honored," he said, offering Connie Wilcox his arm. She grasped it at the elbow and steadied herself. "So are we ready?" Spring asked.

"Ready," she said, looking over at John Lee, who responded with an amused shrug.

So off they went, back across the broad plaza to the arched gateway leading to the Old City. Connie badgered Lucas Spring with questions nearly every step of the way. A step behind the two, John Lee made no attempt to hide his smile. Connie seemed to have forgotten him for the moment, transferring her attention almost completely to her new guide.

He was content to listen as Spring traced the troubled history of the Old City for them. Spring's presentation was polished; he was on familiar territory, having given the tour hundreds of times over the past decade. He quoted the relevant New Testament verses, pointed out the different architectural styles overlaid by centuries of conquest, and offered a few amusing anecdotes from tours he'd given before. Spring was enjoying himself.

By the time they reached the arched doors of the Church of the Holy Sepulchre, John Lee was eager to finish the tour. His eyes were bothering him, stinging from the dryness of the air and the cumulative effects of an afternoon in the sun. He found the church itself depressing, a gloomy place, ornately over-decorated, with clashing architectural styles. The building was crammed with noisy tour groups and too-anxious pilgrims.

Lucas Spring gave them a rushed but comprehensive tour. They climbed the steep steps to Calvary, the "place of the skull," and then Spring guided them through the chapels (Coptic, Latin, and Orthodox), and led them to the atrium, the Chapel of the Angel, and finally, to the tomb itself. They waited in line to enter the sepulcher, a tiny chamber with stone ceilings so low that John Lee and Spring had to hunch over. Each had a few hurried moments to contemplate the marble slab and religious bas reliefs before moving on.

"Doesn't feel like the holiest place in the world, does it?" Connie said to John Lee, somehow sensing his disappointment, when they emerged from the church into the late afternoon sun. They began their walk out of the Christian Quarter, back towards Jerusalem's New City. "I felt that way, too, the first time I came here. You have to get past all that, love. Imagine what happened here. You're in the very spot."

"The Greek Orthodox believe that near the tomb—where they built the Catholicon—is the center of the world," Spring said.

"The Moslems think that it's over at the Dome of the Rock, don't they?" John Lee asked. "So maybe we're in the general vicinity of the center of the universe.

That's going to disappoint a lot of Cowboy fans, because they're convinced that it's on the fifty-yard line of Texas Stadium."

Spring laughed out loud. Connie looked at them blankly, not getting the joke. By then they had neared the walls of the Old City. She was quieter, worn out, John Lee decided, by her long afternoon.

He regretted that he wouldn't be able to describe his surreal tour of the Old City to John Senior. His father would have loved their absurd caravan. It would have struck him as having the makings of a modern Christian parable, an instructive story for a sermon: three strangers, all nursing emotional wounds, thrown together on an odd pilgrimage, ending perfectly (from a theological perspective) when their "walk with Jesus" culminated in the rediscovery of God's forgiveness and grace.

Except it hadn't happened that way. Conveniently spiritual endings occurred in sentimental Sunday homilies, John Lee knew, not in the gritty real world, where he had seen more evidence of divine indifference than divine intervention.

They reached the New Gate and passed through to the crowded, modern street scene waiting outside. Spring hailed one of the passing taxi cabs, which lurched to a stop, barely avoiding a panel van and an ambulance. John Lee helped Connie into the back of the cab as Lucas Spring instructed the driver, already impatient to plunge back into the traffic, about the location of her hotel. They said their good-byes to her— she rewarded John Lee with a kiss on the cheek. Connie Wilcox peered through the back window of the black Mercedes, waving frantically, as the vehicle pulled into heavy traffic and disappeared from view behind a blue-and-white tour group bus.

"You were very kind to help her," Spring said to John Lee.

"Not that kind. If it hadn't been me, it would have been someone else. I'm sure you could see that Connie Wilcox doesn't take no for an answer. She's relentless."

"Nonetheless, your father would have been proud of you," Spring said, and John Lee didn't resent the comment as much as he thought he would. "You know, as unbalanced as she may be, I will tell you that I have to envy her."

"Envy her?"

"Yes," he said. "In a way, I envy her. She takes this place so literally. I envy her certainty, her ability to believe so fiercely, so fully. Did you see her face at the Tomb? How alive it became? She can't get enough of being here."

"The pilgrim from Geelong."

"From where?"

"Geelong. It's her town in Australia. I would bet that it's a one stoplight sort of place. About as far from here as you can get. In every sense."

Spring didn't respond at first. He seemed distracted, lost in his own thoughts.

"I've learned that it's harder here," he said. "That's the amazing part. I thought it'd be the other way around. That there would be a constant validation of my faith here. But it works the other way. You can't rely on your imagination to fill in the biblical blanks, the way you do when you're sitting in your study in Houston or Dallas. When something is grimy, or sordid, you have to confront it."

"I could see some of that today," John Lee said.

"I hope you also sensed a little of the sublime, too."

"A glimmer or two. At the Wall."

"I'm glad I caught up to you. I would have felt guilty, I think, if I hadn't. Otherwise, you would have remembered me as the Philistine more interested in Cowboy scores than in holy places."

"Not me. I've never liked that judgment thing. I'm a preacher's kid, remember? We grow up facing judgment. It gets stale in a hurry."

"Do you want to share a cab back?" Spring asked. "I live in the general direction of your hotel."

"Thanks, but I could use the walk."

"It's a good place to grieve," Spring said offhandedly, almost as if he were talking to himself. "I can speak from personal experience. Grief and sorrow. There's never been a shortage of that here. I think it's in the water supply. You can't get away from it. Thousands of years of it, as a matter of fact. So you picked a good place."

"I didn't pick it. My father did."

"He picked well, then."

"I guess so."

"Jerusalem puts it all in perspective. That's another thing I'll miss, the perspective."

"I see," John Lee said, but he didn't.

The street lights had come on, greeting the dusk, and the beginning of the rush hour had added to the traffic along Hatzanhanim Street. John Lee was tired and wanted to get back to his hotel room and take a hot shower. It would leave him feeling clean. He'd have a few drinks and then write a letter to Maureen about his first day in Jerusalem.

In the morning, he would return to the Old City. He would walk back by himself, clear of distractions, freed from Connie Wilcox's chatter and Lucas Spring's half-submerged sorrow. He could focus, then. Alone, he could more fully honor his father's unstated request and play hide-and-seek with the notion of a Holy Ghost who cared for him and every single soul on the face of the Earth, believers and unbelievers alike.

John Lee would do his best. He would search inside the city's ancient walls and along its narrow streets, hoping that Lucas Spring and T.S. Eliot were right and that prayer was more valid there, trying to stay open to the presence of John Senior's God, to his saving grace, even when, in his heart, he feared he was on a fool's errand. But as his father's only son, it was the least that he could do.

6

The Extraordinary Patience of Things

The snow fell steadily and silently, fashioning a nearly opaque curtain outside the kitchen windows. The softer flakes of early afternoon had thickened with the arrival of colder temperatures, and she wondered if the forecasters on television had been wrong. It looked heavier than the predicted "scattered flurries." By morning, she and Liam were likely to find the neighborhood buried under several feet of wet snow and ice gracing the bare limbs of the black locust and flowering dogwood trees in their backyard.

Liam was late. She sat at the kitchen table with a cup of lukewarm tea and watched the snow begin to cover the bedraggled lawn furniture in the backyard, furniture she had neglected to drag into the garage. Low mounds of snow formed on the seats of the chairs and on the top of the picnic table.

A dusting of white began to cover the branches of the young pine and white cedar trees in the corner of the yard. She and Liam had planted them two years before, when they had made the move to the suburbs and purchased their colonial on Sheffield Street. She remembered how scared she had been by the sudden, adult responsibility of mortgage payments. But there had also been her exhilaration at the prospects of settling down, of finding some permanence.

It was growing darker by the minute. Harder sheets of snow, falling without pause, now completely blocked the weak afternoon sun. She looked to the row of houses beyond the line of oaks in their backyard, and saw that only one had any lights on. She finished her cup of tea. The mug had grown cold to her touch and the last few sips had a cool, milky aftertaste.

The sound of the furnace turning on in the basement startled her. She shivered involuntarily, thinking about how cold it might be outside that night. They had enjoyed a balmy, warmer-than-usual fall with a prolonged Indian summer, and she hadn't welcomed the arrival of cold weather. But she did love the first few hours of a snowstorm, when the snow covered the dingy, late fall landscape with white purity.

She went to the refrigerator and found a half-full bottle of white wine on the bottom shelf, a chardonnay from a Napa Valley winery. It was one of the wines they had bought at the local liquor store after a wine-tasting party in Cambridge a few years before, when Liam had been interested in learning about wines. They had even subscribed to a wine newsletter for a while until Liam realized that Marie didn't really share his enthusiasm for the details of vineyard management. She poured herself a glass and took a long drink. It warmed her throat and stomach. She finished it too quickly and poured another.

Still no sign of Liam. He was usually punctual to a fault. Liam could be counted on to be on time. Marie wasn't as reliable herself. The snow must be snarling the early evening rush hour traffic, she decided, delaying his return home.

She turned on the radio on the counter. One of Mozart's piano concertos was playing on her favorite classical music station. She tried listening, but the majesty of the music, its precision and clarity, somehow made her feel insignificant and sad. She didn't want to start crying again, so she turned the radio off. Besides, she wanted to listen for the sound of Liam's car coming down the driveway. She fought the temptation to look out at the driveway, remembering her grandmother's cliché about a watched pot never boiling. She wondered whether it held true for a watched driveway.

The snow must have muffled the sounds of his tires on gravel, because she only first heard him stamping his boots on the back mat, clearing them of snow. He carefully placed his leather briefcase on the floor and pulled off his trench coat, hanging it in the corner closet. He was impatient to be inside, in the warmth and light of the kitchen.

"Hey," he said in greeting. "It's really coming down, now. Route 128 is a mess. A lot of spinouts. Slow going all the way. That's why I'm late."

"It's not supposed to be more than a couple of inches," she said. "That's all they forecast."

"Another lousy forecast from our crack local TV weatherguys. They should try throwing darts or using chicken bones and dice. They'd probably get better results."

He looked over at the wine bottle on the kitchen table and her half-finished glass. There was a quarter of the bottle left.

"Would you like a glass of wine?" she asked, seeing his glance.

"No," he said. "Not right now."

"How was work?"

"Same old same old," he said. "For the most part." He joined her at the kitchen table. "But we closed two searches today. A real top-notch group of candidates. Experienced, technologically savvy. One of them is sure to get placed. Bruce is really pleased, and he thinks it'll mean a lot more business next year."

She nodded, feigning an interest in Liam's work that was deeper than she really felt at the moment. She was glad that Liam enjoyed what he did for a living, the challenge of finding the right candidate, of calling strangers and trying to persuade them to interview for a new position in an unfamiliar company. Liam was very good at it, which surprised Marie, because she hadn't ever thought of him as a salesman.

"How was your day?" he asked.

"Very quiet," she said, deciding to wait before talking about her afternoon. "Felicia Bainbridge called this morning." She tried to keep her tone neutral, matter-of-fact. Liam didn't like Felicia.

"Did she?"

"She invited us over to their place in two weeks. A Saturday. There are two other couples coming."

"What's the occasion?" he asked.

"No occasion. Felicia is just being social. You know we haven't seen them in months."

"I thought you had lunch with her a couple of weeks ago."

"I did. We went to a Mexican place in Cambridge, on Mass Ave. We must have had three Margaritas each and two baskets of those tortilla chips. We had a great time."

"But we haven't seen them since the summer," she continued. "We as a couple, I mean. Phil's been traveling a lot this fall, and Felicia said this was the first clear weekend in a while."

"Who are the other people she has invited?"

"I think they're both from Felicia's neighborhood in Cambridge."

"Great," he said, drawing out the word in the slow way he did when he was annoyed. "I can see I'm going to fit in perfectly. Perfectly."

"Your enthusiasm is infectious."

"Sorry. I don't mean to be a jerk, but you know that I don't have a lot in common with Felicia Bainbridge. Or Phil Bainbridge. Their friends are going to have similar interests. I know you like Felicia and she's a good friend, but I always feel two steps behind in the conversation."

"That's not so," she said. "I don't see that at all."

"We don't have a lot in common," he said. "I mean, I don't have a lot in common with them."

Liam felt uncomfortable around her friends from graduate school, especially the more affluent ones. She tried to be patient about his insecurities. Liam remained convinced that he didn't fit in, no matter how many times she reassured him that he did.

"I thought it might be a chance for us to get out," she said. "Otherwise, I'm going to go crazy. Stir crazy, isn't that what it's called?"

"That's it," he said. "Stir is slang for prison. It's going crazy over being confined."

"How did you know that?"

"I read it in a slang dictionary once," he said.

"You know the strangest things."

"One of my hidden strengths."

"I think we could have a great time with Felicia and Phil," she said. "We'll meet some new people as well."

"You're right," he said, relenting, his tone softening. "It will get us out. So let's go. And I'll do my best to be charming and witty. You'll have to remind me of the names of all those ski resorts in Colorado that Felicia always seems to be visiting."

"Don't agree to go just on my account," she said.

"Isn't that a good reason?" he asked. "A valid one?"

"Perhaps for you," she said. "But I don't want you to feel that you're being dragged to Felicia's kicking and screaming."

"No screaming," he said, smiling at her. "You won't have to drag me there. I promise."

"Okay," she said.

"What are we going to do about Christmas?" he asked. "It's only three weeks away and Sean has been asking."

They had been to her brother's house in Baltimore for Thanksgiving and so, she knew, Liam expected that she would agree to visit his brother on Christmas. Marie had hoped that somehow they could beg off, because she didn't find the Callinan clan's Thanksgiving or Christmas gatherings to be relaxing, or particularly welcoming.

Liam's family had never warmed up to her; they saw her as an outsider. Marie wasn't Catholic, her family hadn't originally immigrated from Ireland, she hadn't been born at St. Margaret's Hospital, nor had she grown up in a triple-decker in Dorchester playing with the other neighborhood kids in McConnell or Savin Hill Park or on Malibu Beach. She didn't share the Callinan memories of Christmas Eve midnight mass at St. William's.

Even though Liam's brothers and sister had settled in comfortable suburbs like Hingham and Norwell and all had good jobs—Sean was a stockbroker, Colin a certified public accountant, and Grace a cardiac nurse at Mass General—they were still clannish, and fiercely proud, about where they had come from. Marie wasn't O.F.D.—Originally From Dorchester—and there was no way to alter that. They wouldn't ever fully include her. Alone among the Callinans Liam didn't seem to care about the old neighborhood, but he did care about joining his family for the holidays.

"I don't know," she said. "We'd talked about having Christmas alone. Just the two of us."

He didn't respond. He crossed his arms, closed off in wordless annoyance.

"Can we talk about it more?" she asked. "I'm not sure yet."

"What aren't you sure about? You want me to find time for Felicia's dinner party, but we're going to put Sean and Jean off, and they're family. At Christmas."

"I don't want to fight," she said.

"I'm not looking to fight," he said.

"You could have fooled me."

"It's just that my family will expect us. I think Sean will be hurt if we turn him down when we're staying here. It's different when we're away for Christmas."

She knew Liam was right about Sean. He'd take it personally if they didn't join them for Christmas, see it as a snub. She would be blamed, of course. Sean's Irish paranoia was the worst in the family. Liam had joked once that Sean believed that most of the world, outside his tight circle of family and friends, secretly wore orange underwear on St. Patrick's Day. Marie didn't really understand that sense of persecution. She had grown up in a sedate little town in Maryland outside Annapolis where no one seemed overly passionate about anything.

They had spent one Christmas in the Bahamas, the first year they were married. Marie loved being away from the cold, fleeing that year's dismal December rain for the sun and warmth of Nassau. It had been carefree and romantic, a second honeymoon, and she hadn't missed the traditional Christmas celebrations at all.

But when they got back to Boston, Sean and Colin had needled Liam about the trip at the next family gathering, at Sean's house in Hingham, on New Year's Day. "Liam, the jet-setter," Sean began. "Club Med, was it, over the Christmas break? The Caribbean? A wicked good vacation spot."

"The Bahamas," said Liam. "Nassau. Not Club Med."

"Excuse me," Sean said, and then with the broadest South Boston accent he could manufacture. "The Bah-hah-mas." They all laughed and Liam just shook his head. Liam's own accent surfaced only when he was tired or angry or under stress. Marie had teased him once that if Boston was cut off from the rest of the country for fifty years, no one would believe that the locals were still speaking English.

"Lay off him," Colin said. "He needs that January tan to impress his clients."

Sean wasn't done, though. "Will his schedule let him join his brothers for a Bruins game in a couple of weeks?" he asked, using the English pronunciation of "schedule," provoking more laughter. "Can he fit us in between his international trips?"

"Hey," said Liam. "Wait a minute. You're the Wall Street stock market hotshot. You're the one with the hefty net worth. I can't help it if you're so tight that you can't bring yourself to spend any of it. Jean's wanted to take a vacation someplace warm for years. And she's not thinking of Brewster."

Colin sputtered with laughter. "He nailed you," he said to Sean. "Admit it. Someplace warm, but not Brewster. That's priceless." Sean had purchased a Cape summer home in Brewster five years before, but it was a joke in the family how reluctantly he'd made the investment.

Marie had loved the banter between Liam and his brothers. She wasn't witty herself and she was attracted to their dark, Celtic humor, even if Sean's joking implied a criticism of her influence on Liam. She just wanted the Callinan byplay in smaller doses than did Liam.

She didn't respond to Liam's question about their Christmas plans, and, impatient, he went upstairs to change. Marie finished her glass of wine and then emptied what was left in the bottle into her glass. She didn't want to face Liam's disapproving look when he returned, so she put the empty bottle back into the refrigerator. She positioned it behind the milk where he would have to take it out to realize that it was empty. She'd dump it in the trash the next morning, after he'd gone to work.

She began preparing omelettes for their dinner. She heard the sound of the shower upstairs. She made their omelettes swiftly, chopping the cheddar cheese, tomatoes and leeks, and then folding those ingredients into the eggs she was cooking on her big cast-iron skillet. Meanwhile, their English muffins were browning in the toaster oven. She made Liam a cup of instant coffee. She felt slightly dizzy from the wine.

He came down the back steps to the kitchen, his hair still wet from the shower. He had changed out of his navy blazer and gray flannel trousers into jeans and a turtleneck. Liam looked fit in his casual clothing. He was proud of his trim waistline, the product of weekend running and weight-lifting twice a week over at the YMCA fitness center.

They sat down at the kitchen table and she served the food. Liam gave her a wan smile. She knew he wouldn't question her about Sean's invitation again.

"One of my favorites," he said, pleased. "I could smell the eggs cooking upstairs. I'm starved."

"Can I get you anything else?" she asked.

"How about a glass of that wine now?"

"We don't have anything really cold," she said, embarrassed. "Do you mind some at room temperature?"

"That would be fine," he said.

She went to the kitchen closet and found another bottle of the chardonnay. Fortunately it was cold just from contact with the outside wall. She poured him a glass and was tempted to add to hers, but knew it would bother Liam, so she didn't. They ate at the kitchen table, silently.

They were near the end of the dinner—she had finished her omelette and was sipping a cup of tea—when she described her afternoon. She had started a new decorating project, scraping the wallpaper from the upstairs bathroom walls. Her plan was to repaint the walls in an oil-based enamel. She had gone to the paint store and picked out Dutch Boy Shaker White, a more subtle color.

"I scraped about half the wall," she said.

"I saw when I was taking my shower."

"Halfway through I started crying," she said. "It was a sad song on the radio I was listening to. I know it's irrational but I couldn't help myself."

"It made you cry?" He put down his fork, disturbed.

"It doesn't take much. I couldn't stop for about twenty minutes. I gave up doing any more scraping."

"You're still fragile," he said. "Hell, I'm still fragile."

"I don't like feeling like this," she said. "I'm sorry to bring you down with me. I need to stop dwelling on it. It's not fair to you."

"Don't be absurd," he said. "It's not a matter of fairness. Whatever you're feeling matters to me because I love you and we're in this together."

"I want to try again," she said. "I'm willing to try. I decided that today. Doctor Attasian said at my last appointment that we could begin trying again, that my body is ready now."

"That's great. That you want to try. But don't you think we should wait? It'd probably be easier on you if we waited a bit."

"Easier?"

"And safer. I don't want to see you disappointed or hurt again."

"So what am I supposed to do? While we're waiting?"

"Why don't you go back to school? Take some courses? Or you could find a job. Or do whatever interests you."

"Those are your solutions," she told him. "That might make sense for you, but not for me."

"At least they're a start. They get you moving forward."

"I'm not sure I want to move forward, if that's what you think moving forward is."

"Then what do you want to do?"

"I told you."

"Other than that."

"I don't know. I feel flat," she said. "Most of the time, I don't feel much of anything. I don't get angry or passionate or upset. The days just go by, and I'm just hoping to get through them."

She was tired of talking. She knew Liam would want to figure out a "solution," and she dreaded that conversation. She didn't believe in solutions any more. It was where they differed. She accepted the randomness of life, the sudden ups and downs, and he wouldn't.

"I'm sorry to hear that," he said. "I was hoping things had gotten better. From before."

"They have," she lied. "Some."

"It's going to take time."

"I know," she said. She cleared their plates and placed them in the sink. She washed her hands and dried them with paper toweling.

"I'm going for a walk," she announced.

"Do you want some company?" he asked.

"No," she said. "I'd like to be alone."

Liam nodded, already expecting the response. When she was upset, Marie took walks by herself. She pulled on a fleece vest and parka and added a ski cap and gloves, prepared for the weather.

Outside it was warmer than she'd expected, the falling snow giving the air a soft, moist feel. She decided that she would walk a long way. She hoped that she could empty her mind, that she could think of nothing but the whiteness of the snow and the hush of the night around her.

She began moving ahead, finding her way more by instinct than by conscious navigation, aware of her breathing and the perspiration that gathered under her shirt as she trudged forward.

She looked at her watch. To her surprise, she discovered that she had been out for an hour, oblivious to the time. She had walked through the town center, past the Commons and then west by the pond and the new middle school. Then she doubled back through the recently completed townhouse development where many of the houses had family rooms with cathedral ceilings and five bedrooms and three baths and were already covered with Christmas lights, until she reached the edge of her neighborhood. To the west was a large open expanse of fields, the outside boundaries of a local nature preserve, and a dark stand of trees. Snow covered the ground although it was dark and hard to see because the only illumination came from the streetlights.

She thought about how she could wander off into the woods and vanish, disappearing from the life she was leading. How long before Liam reported her missing? Would the police find her tracks heading across the field? Would they mount a search, bringing in dogs and helicopters to scour the surrounding nature preserve? Would the detectives suspect Liam of "foul play," of having killed her and hidden the body? Would anyone think she had fled to California or Mexico, escaping the winter chill and her current life? What would the neighbors say? And her friends? She found herself grinning at the absurdity of it.

She walked back down the street and turned the corner at Sheffield. From there she could see the living room windows of their house. Reflected blue light from their television set flickered on the window. Liam must have grown bored while waiting for her return. He would be on the recliner, his feet propped up, watching television and glancing through the *Globe*. On most nights she would be there too, on the nearby couch, with her latest book or cross-stitching, usually ignoring whatever was on the television, content to just be there. Occasionally Liam would find something of interest in the newspaper and read it out loud to her, but for the most part they didn't talk, content with the comfortable proximity.

Marie had been exploring poetry again. She had paperbacks of verse by Adrienne Rich, John Ashbury, and Gary Snyder on the corner table. She had been reading Robinson Jeffers, as well, and just within the week had been struck by a poem of his, "Carmel Point," and its opening line, "The extraordinary patience of things." She had wondered what he had been driving at, because the words couldn't mean anything in a literal sense. How could things be patient? Or better yet, why would things be *extraordinarily* patient? Marie loved the ambiguity of the poem. She longed for that patience, the quiet, nonjudgmental patience of things.

She had no wish to go back inside the house just yet. She stood at the edge of the street, lost in thought, mesmerized by the lights, and then was startled by her name being called. She looked up and saw a Volvo station wagon stopped in the street, its brake lights on and the window rolled down.

She saw that the driver was Mr. Perkins, the earnest man who lived in the powder-blue colonial up the street, the only house in the neighborhood with a wrap-around porch. She remembered that he had something to do with software and computers and that he loved to garden. In the spring, he was the first on their street to start ministering to flower beds and shrubs ravaged by the New England winter.

"Marie?" he called. "Is that you, Marie?"

"It's me," she called back. "It's Marie."

He put the station wagon in reverse and slowly, cautiously, rolled back, bringing the car to a stop so that the front driver's side window was parallel with her. "Is everything all right?" he asked, peering at her through the snow.

"Yes," she said. "I'm fine."

"I saw someone standing there and not moving and I thought..." Perkins let his words trail off. "I thought it was you but I wasn't sure."

"It's me," she said. "I'm just enjoying the quiet and the snow. Thanks for stopping, but there's nothing to worry about."

"Looks like we're getting more snow than we bargained for."

"That we are," she said. "Every time it snows I think about how we were taught in grammar school that the Eskimos have thirty-five different words for snow. But the truth is that they don't. They have just one, like us. Liam researched that when he was in college. Another one of those popular myths that isn't true."

"I didn't know that," he said politely, but Marie could see that he was puzzled. She had just wanted to make conversation, to reassure him that she was all right.

"Thanks for stopping," she said, repeating herself. "I don't want to keep you."

"Fine," he said, relieved that he had done the neighborly thing and could continue on his way, his conscience clear. "I'm sorry if I startled you. Take care, then." He rolled up the window and slowly pulled away, the tire treads leaving a fresh pattern in the snow.

She stood there, watching Mr. Perkins' station wagon with its "Visualize Peace" bumper sticker and the Martha's Vineyard parking decals on the back window slowly negotiate its way down the street and then disappear into the snow. He would probably remark to his wife Chloe that he had found Marie standing in the street, and Chloe, a sharp, hard-edged woman with a demanding career of her own, would no doubt conclude that Marie and Liam were having problems. Not the first, nor the last, couple in their neighborhood with problems.

The Lanigans, who had lived four houses up the street, had divorced a year ago. First there had been a trial separation, with Bryce Lanigan moving out of the house. Months later Marie had seen him at the Star Market, grocery shopping by himself with a haggard and lost look, like he hadn't had a decent meal in weeks. Marie had heard from Chloe Perkins that Renee Lanigan's doubles tennis partner, a young woman who had also divorced her husband, had been staying with Renee. Chloe had commented about how "unusual" Renee's relationship with her friend seemed, but Marie had ignored her and had changed the subject. Before too long, the Lanigans were gone. They sold their house to a young orthopedic surgeon affiliated with Children's Hospital, finalized their divorce, and disappeared from Sheffield Street and the town.

She thought about the snow piling up on the front walk and the driveway. In the morning she would get up before Liam and head outside and shovel the driveway clean so he could get his car out. She looked forward to that, to losing herself in hard, physical work, in the half-hour or so it would take to clear the snow down to the dark asphalt.

She felt as if she could see and hear more clearly. She thought she could hear the downward rushing of the snow, making a hissing sound so faint that she wondered if she was imagining it. Did snow have a sound? *That would be a good Robinson Jeffers' poem*, she thought. Then she heard the sound of the wind moving the trees in their backyard, the hint of creaking branches, the feel of snow blown onto her face, a cool mist.

She opened her mouth and impulsively stuck out her tongue. She caught a few snowflakes on her it, enjoying the sudden wetness, and delighting in the childishness of the gesture. She decided that she would wait until Liam was asleep before she re-entered the house. She didn't mind waiting.

7

Morning in America

From nearly half a block away she could make out the Garbers' living room, bright with lights, a beacon of sorts on the quiet suburban street. Adrienne tugged on Beau's arm and pointed out their destination. As they drew closer, they could hear the sounds of animated conversation and the soft strains of Pachabel's Canon. For once during their walk, she didn't have to struggle to match Beau's longer stride as he had noticeably slackened his pace as they walked up Murray Place and moved closer to the Garbers' house.

Adrienne had enjoyed their stroll down Nassau Street and their detour through Princeton's hushed side streets, the still-colorful maples and oaks forming a brilliant autumnal canopy above them. Beau had reluctantly agreed to attend the Garbers' dinner party only as a favor to Adrienne. She'd asked him to substitute for her boyfriend, Hugh, who had to stay over in Chicago another day on business to finish some involved negotiations.

Anyone watching them make their way down the street would think they were a handsome couple, she decided, a well matched couple. Next to Beau, she didn't feel that her legs were too long. It made her wish Hugh had Beau's lanky frame, and then she felt guilty for entertaining the thought. A friend of hers, a fellow dancer, had once observed, with more than a touch of jealousy, that Adrienne had been blessed with a Balanchine body, elongated but sinuous. But those same long legs had made Adrienne prone to injury, and a stress fracture in her right foot that never healed properly had ended her career as a performer and left her to make a living as a teacher and choreographer.

Beau had been in town for a week on a rare visit to his parents. Even though she hadn't seen him in two years, she didn't hesitate in asking him to accompany her. They'd always been direct with each other, and, unlike some of her friends, she had never been intimidated by Beau.

"I've cancelled on Zoe Garber twice," she had explained to him. "Bailed out on other invitations to dinner. So I really need to go, or she's going to think I'm avoiding her, or that I'm holding some sort of grudge."

"Can't you go solo?" he asked. "Where do I come in? Why do you need me to go?"

"Because it's a dinner party with couples," she said. "There's the Garbers, Zoe and her husband, Levi, who's a journalist. He's on a sabbatical of sorts to write a book on Congress and Zoe's very active in local politics. And then there's another couple, Derek and Gillian Hawthorne. They're English. He's a visiting professor, in mathematics, I think, and she designs jewelry. We'd be the third couple."

"But we're not a couple."

"We are and we're not," she said. "You're not my boyfriend, but you'll balance the table. You know, boy girl, boy girl. So I need you along. Please, Beau, as a favor."

"I don't think I'll really fit in with your friends."

"Sure you will," she said. "Besides, Julia told me that your parents have to attend some faculty function Saturday night, so you're going to be free. Don't tell me you have a better offer because I know it's not so."

"I was thinking of catching a movie at the Garden," he said. "You're welcome to come along."

"But I really need you at the Garbers," she said. "You're always so clever and well-informed. You'll carry the conversation for us if they want to talk about politics or the economy."

"Was that supposed to be Hugh's job?"

"Of course," she said. "You know how it bores me. If they want to talk about Baryshnikov or Martens, that's different. I doubt I'll be that lucky."

"You'd consider these friends of yours to be intellectuals, wouldn't you?" he asked, and she remembered that Beau had never had much patience for academics—probably a reflection of his troubled relationship with his father.

"No," she said. "Not in the way you mean. They're relatively normal. Beau, you should come. It'll take your mind off things."

"What things?" he asked. "I didn't realize I needed to be distracted."

"I know it's difficult when you come back," she said. "With your parents."

He paused for a long moment. "It can be tough. I don't know how Jimmy and Julia handle living so close to the Professor. I can't believe I'm the only one he picks arguments with."

"It's probably because he misses you," she said. "Maybe you're the only one who will fight with him."

"You always do try to find the positive," he said. "As long as I've known you, you've been that way."

"Whatever other way is there? Come to the dinner with me. I promise you won't be bored."

In the end he agreed to go to the dinner party with her. When she called Zoe Garber, Adrienne explained that Beau was an old Princeton friend, that he was well-traveled, had broad interests, and could carry his end of a conversation.

"Should Hugh be jealous?" Zoe asked.

"Lord, no," Adrienne said. "There's absolutely no danger of that."

"Is he gay then?"

Adrienne laughed at the thought. "Beau Kincaid? I can assure you, personally, that's not the case."

"I see."

"It was a long time ago," Adrienne said. "Ages ago. A college thing."

It was Zoe who met them at the front door. A thin, intense woman in her early thirties, she wore her light red hair pinned in a bun. Her lightly freckled face made her look much younger than her husband, Levi Garber, who had grown a beard to compensate for his receding hairline. Levi shook hands with both of them in welcome, nodding to Beau. Zoe hugged Adrienne, complimenting her dress, and offered her hand to Beau, openly appraising him.

Zoe then introduced them to their other guests, the Hawthornes, who stood awkwardly by the door with half-empty wine glasses.

"Beau! What a marvelous name," Gillian Hawthorne said. She wore a white peasant blouse and dark wrap-around skirt. Silver and turquoise bracelets and a silver choker necklace completed her outfit. "Beau Kincaid. I don't think I've met a Beau before."

"That's not his given name," Adrienne said. "Just his nickname. His real name is Wilson."

"So how did you come to be called Beau?" asked Zoe, turning to Beau.

Beau smiled. "I'm sure Adrienne can explain. She'll tell the story much better."

"Beau is the oldest of three brothers," Adrienne said. "Remember the brothers in the movie *Beau Geste*? In the movie Beau is the oldest, always leading the other two. I think it was my friend Julia King who began calling him Beau. It certainly fit him better than Wilson."

"It was Julia," Beau said, "So there you have it. All of my secrets exposed in the first five minutes you've known me. Thank you, Adrienne. Perhaps we can turn to something more interesting than my childhood."

"Beau, you'll always interest me," Adrienne said. "Even your childhood interests me."

"So you have known each other for a long time?" It was Levi Garber, curious about their easy familiarity.

"Since we were kids," Adrienne said. "Beau and I were an item once, when he was a senior in college and I was a freshman. It didn't last, although I did my best. I'm afraid that Beau has a reputation for a short attention span. Julia was luckier than me, she married a Kincaid, Beau's brother, Jimmy."

"That's not the whole story, of course," Beau said. "Adrienne loves to tease me. But I'll spare you the details, so you're not bored senseless about our childhood romances."

They had been together for a summer, Adrienne realized. She remembered how she had been attracted by his toughness and irreverence—so different from the other college boys—and by his unabashed maleness. Beau was definitely out of step with the times, a throwback. While most of his contemporaries seemed to be dodging the draft or finding reasons for avoiding military service, Beau had turned up one Christmas in uniform. He had joined ROTC at the University of Virginia and when he graduated he had become an Army officer. She had found that intriguing. Many of her friends at the time despised Beau for it, but it didn't bother her, because she wasn't particularly political.

They had corresponded for a while during his senior year, and sporadically during his first few months in flight school at Fort Rucker, but she realized that she had no hold over him. The only reason they had stayed in touch over the years was because her best friend, Julia, had married Beau's younger brother Jimmy.

Levi appeared at Adrienne's shoulder and offered her, and then Beau, a glass of Sauvignon Blanc. Zoe encouraged them to move into the living room and sit down. It was an inviting room, comfortable in a spare way. On the far wall light oak built-in bookshelves were crammed with hardback books—serious books, biographies of world leaders, political memoirs, a few volumes on journalism, and an embossed crimson-and-gold set of the *Harvard Classics*. A thick braided rug covered the gleaming polished oak floor. Beau and Adrienne sat down on one of the two Scandinavian-style couches and the Hawthornes occupied the other. Levi and Zoe sat facing them in armless teak chairs.

Derek Hawthorne broke his prolonged silence by asking Levi to finish a story he'd started about covering Congress as Washington bureau chief for a newspaper chain based in the Midwest. Derek had a neatly-trimmed mustache and he wore round, wire-framed glasses. Levi smoothly picked up his narrative, explaining how he'd exposed the taxpayer-financed Caribbean junkets of a Wisconsin Congressman who was stupid enough to take his wife and mistress to the same hotel in Jamaica on consecutive weekends.

"He signed them both in as Mrs. Gustafson," Levi said. "When my story broke in his hometown paper, he was more worried about what the real Mrs. Gustafson would do than about any action of the House Ethics Committee."

"Is he still in Congress?" asked Derek. He had what Adrienne would have described as an Oxbridge accent, clipped and precise, clearly upper class.

"Of course," Levi said. "His constituents were very forgiving. More than Mrs. Gustafson. Representative Gustafson had delivered a federal building project or two to the district."

"What did his wife do about it?" Gillian asked.

"Divorced him. And then signed on as the campaign manager for her ex-husband's opponent in the primary. Gustafson came within five hundred votes of losing his seat. But he held on."

"What about the other woman?" It was Gillian again.

"She disappeared. At least from public view."

His story completed, Levi excused himself to check the progress of dinner. "I'm the chef tonight," he explained.

"You don't realize how lucky you are," Zoe told them. "Levi's clearly the best cook in the Garber family."

The conversation shifted to a vacation the Hawthornes were planning to take to the Greek islands in the spring.

"Mykanos," Zoe said. "Be sure to visit Mykanos. And Tinos and Siros and Santorini, too, if you can spare the time."

"Have you been to Greece?" Derek asked, including both Beau and Adrienne in his question.

"I have," Adrienne said. "But to Athens, not the islands."

"Can't say I have," Beau said.

"Oh, you should go," Gillian said emphatically. "I get so many ideas for my jewelry by traveling to new places. If you can open yourself to newness, there is so much to discover."

"I live in San Diego," Beau said. "Sometime I think that's all we have there. Newness. You know they say we're a year ahead of the rest of the country."

Adrienne couldn't help but giggle at that. "Have you opened yourself to newness, Beau?"

"I'm working on it," he said, amused, enjoying her sudden playfulness. "I've got to learn some new tricks."

"What's wrong with the old tricks?" asked Gillian, trying to keep pace. Adrienne noticed that her accent was broader than her husband's and she swallowed her vowels more.

"Nothing," he said. "Except Adrienne knows them all."

"That I do," she said. "I guess they're not as effective for Beau as they were in the Steve Canyon days."

"Steve Canyon?" Gillian asked. "Who is that?" She seemed mystified, and Adrienne was secretly pleased.

"A private joke," Beau said. "Adrienne is trying to provoke me tonight and I'm going to ignore her."

They were interrupted by the return of Levi, who invited them to bring their drinks and move into the dining room. Zoe seated Beau and Gillian on one side of the table and Adrienne and Derek on the other; she and Levi occupied the end chairs.

"There was this ghastly parade in London last week celebrating the Falklands victory," Derek began as Levi served them the appetizer, an Oriental salad with tangerines. "If you can call it that. All those poor blokes killed for a stupid island at the end of the world so Thatcher can boast that we still have an empire."

"My brother told me that the crowd was estimated at half a million," Gillian said.

"It's a sad commentary on what we celebrate," Derek said.

"Speaking of sad commentaries," Levi said. "Did you hear that the University has invited Al Haig to visit here as a lecturer?"

Derek shook his head. "You'd think the administration would realize how offensive that is to many in the University community. Not only are his politics amoral, but the man has no academic credentials to speak of."

"He's that awful 'I'm in control' man, isn't he?" asked Gillian. "When Reagan was shot. It had the ring of the putsch, didn't it? 'I'm in control.' Quite horrid."

"That was Al Haig," Levi said. "Now he's out of the administration. Forced out, I hear."

"What do you think?" Zoe asked Beau directly. "About the Haig invitation?"

"I hadn't been following it that closely," Beau said. "I'd categorize that as political, and I don't think of myself as being very political."

"I'm not either," Adrienne said. "I try to avoid politics if I can. It makes me mellower when I do."

"I am political," Zoe said, proudly. "More so than Levi, who is supposed to be objective, whatever that means."

"I'm somewhere in between you," Gillian said. "I do have my causes, like the environment and peace. But I don't care for politicians at all."

They had finished their salads and Levi brought out the main course of chicken breasts in Alfredo sauce, with pasta and baby carrots. He beamed when they complimented his cooking.

Derek hadn't finished with politics. "I'd be gratified, and I think most Europeans would be gratified, if you would come to your senses and get Reagan out of the White House," he began. "It's something I just don't understand about the US, why Reagan engenders such support."

"We'll have another chance soon enough," Levi said. "I think that if Anderson hadn't run this last time Carter could have held on. The country will have a clear choice in the next election. If the Democrats put up a half-decent candidate, and the economy stays in this recession, I think they can take back the White House."

Derek frowned. "But in the meantime, the rest of us have to live with the consequences of Reagan's brinksmanship. This madness with the cruise and Pershing missiles in Germany. You can't blame the Soviets for seeing the American position as a provocation. A flexing of muscles. It raises the tensions to a very dangerous level. You can understand why the nuclear freeze movement has swept Europe. We have no desire to be held hostage by the macho cowboy policies of Washington."

"You know many of us in this country are just as dismayed," Levi said.

"We're not all Neanderthals," his wife added.

"And this amazing gambit with Star Wars," Derek said, warming to his topic. He could see he had an appreciative audience in the Garbers. "Billions of dollars for a concept no credible scientist thinks can ever work and that further exacerbates Soviet paranoia about the US."

"I'm afraid there's been a lot of wounded American pride to repair," Levi said. "The Iran hostage situation. The Japanese passing us by economically. Rattling the sword makes some people feel more secure."

"It's just bullying," Zoe said. "No different than kids in a schoolyard."

Levi saw that Beau and Adrienne had yet to join the conversation and he made an effort to draw them in. Adrienne could see that Beau had leaned away from the table and she wondered whether Levi would recognize the clear message he was sending with his body language.

"So what do you think, Beau?" Levi asked. "What are your views on these foreign policy issues? I suspect even non-political types may have opinions on America's role."

"Beau is ex-military," Adrienne said with defensive haste. She hoped to keep Beau from being drawn into the conversation. "A pilot. I probably should have said something earlier."

"Not at all," Levi said. "He's entitled to his own opinion. I've met some very progressive people with service backgrounds. Admiral Gene LaRoque, for instance. He's supporting the nuclear freeze."

"Not me," Beau said. "I guess I'm not very progressive."

"You're not," Levi said, slightly embarrassed. He looked over at Adrienne, unsure of himself for the first time that evening.

"I don't have an opinion," Adrienne said. "One way or the other."

Gillian leaned forward, her face flush from the wine, her eyes fixed on Beau. "Are you a cold warrior, then?" she asked, an undercurrent of hostility in her tone. "You look to me like a bona fide warrior. It's the way you carry yourself. I can tell."

Beau looked at her curiously, unsure of her motives. "I'm not sure what you mean," he said gently.

"I divide the world of men into several camps," she said. "Warriors fall into one of those camps. They have a long history. Perhaps the second oldest profession." She laughed. "They have tough faces and big muscles, always ready for conflict. The first stage of human evolution."

Derek muttered something about rubbish under his breath.

"Gillian has her theories," Zoe said. She gave Adrienne a quick glance. "I'm sure Beau would cop to the muscles."

"I don't know what the other camps are, but I guess at one time in my life I would have been considered a warrior," Beau said. "I'll admit to that. But I'm no longer in the military. Thankfully, I should say."

"Ah, then you have the opportunity to switch camps," Gillian said. "To become a man of letters, or even become a lover." She giggled. "Not a bad trade, that. Isn't that what they do with successful race horses? They go from warrior to lover. They put them out to stud, I think that's the term."

"That's enough conjecture for tonight," Derek said. "I think Beau should be left alone in whatever camp he prefers."

"I don't think of Beau as a joiner," Adrienne said. "I think he's more resistant to change than anyone I know. He's too stubborn."

"What do you think?" Zoe asked Beau, clearly annoyed at Adrienne's interruption. She also liked to know where her guests stood. "About the situation in Europe."

"The situation in Europe," repeated Beau. He considered his response for a moment, clearly reluctant to engage it. "That's a complex question."

"Not that complex," she said, a slight edge in her voice.

Beau glanced over at Adrienne, looking for help. She sensed that he was willing to dodge the issue, to steer the conversation back to lighter topics, if that was what she wanted.

"They are all ears," she said to him. "Wouldn't want you to let down the side—the warrior side, that is."

"It's easier on the domestic front," Beau said. "I'm not crazy about President Reagan's domestic policies. I can do without them. But I can't quarrel with his approach towards Ivan."

"Ivan?" asked Gillian. "Who is Ivan?"

"The Russians," her husband explained, looking at Beau. "Beau is a cold warrior, it seems."

Beau looked across the table at Adrienne and shrugged. She suddenly regretted having brought him—it was a mistake. She should have gone to the movies with him.

"I mean, don't you agree it's time we moved beyond this male fixation with power before it leads to a catastrophe?" Gillian asked, fixing her eyes on Beau.

"I wouldn't know where to begin with that," he said. He turned to Adrienne and opened his hands in a gesture of resignation, ignoring the others. "This is why I don't come back very often. I told you I don't fit in here."

"You seem to be holding your own," she said.

Derek seemed annoyed with his wife. He glared at her, and then turned his attention back to Beau.

"Does that mean you agree with the cowboy tactics of Reagan?" he asked, his pitch slightly higher.

"President Reagan," Beau corrected him. "I don't endorse everything he's done. But from what I can gather, he's right about the Pershing and cruise missiles. The Soviets have been testing us with the deployment of the SS-20 in Eastern Europe. Three-warheads each missile. If they'll forgo them, then we won't put the Pershings in. Seems like a fair trade to me."

"I don't see it in those terms," Derek said. "We come back to the inescapable fact that it is the US introducing theater nuclear weapons. The Soviets have offered to freeze the situation, to keep nuclear weapons out of continental Europe."

"That's the Soviet propaganda machine," Beau said. "They started the escalation with their SS-20s."

"No," Derek said, his voice wavering slightly."I can't agree with that."

Derek seemed caught off guard by Beau's willingness to contest his views. Adrienne guessed that Derek wasn't used to being contradicted. He reminded her of an almost-famous choreographer she had worked with years before, a Russian named Gregor who wouldn't listen to suggestions. Adrienne knew the troupe, knew what they could and couldn't do gracefully, but Gregor expected his steps to be danced his way, without any modifications.

Derek's face was flushed. "People of good will fault your country for the escalation. The cruise, the Pershing, now the MX. It upsets the balance of power, in a destabilizing way, just as Star Wars does, even if it's technically pure folly. It is an unspeakable gamble on your part, risking all of our lives."

Beau considered Derek's response for a moment. "I'll confess I have my doubts about the technical aspects of SDI, what you're calling Star Wars, but hell, if it's fatally flawed, then why are the Soviets so frantic to stop it? If it isn't going to work, then you'd think they would be happy to let us spend ourselves into bankruptcy."

"You're serious," Zoe said, incredulously, and Adrienne saw that she was clenching her fists. She looked over and made eye contact with Adrienne, arching her eyebrows in disgust. Adrienne glanced away, refusing to acknowledge the gesture, feeling that to do so would somehow be an act of disloyalty to Beau.

"You're serious," Zoe repeated.

"Of course I'm serious," Beau said. "President Reagan may not make the career diplomatic types at the State Department happy, but it seems to me that he's a hell of a negotiator."

"If we make it through this period of madness," Derek said, "historians will look back and assign the majority of the blame for the Cold War, and this insane arms race, to America."

"We ought to change subjects, shouldn't we?" Adrienne asked. She turned to Zoe for help. "I don't think anyone's going to change their minds tonight. There's no point in becoming emotional over this. We can agree to disagree, can't we?"

Zoe remained silent, apparently willing to let the argument continue. Adrienne thought that it might be because Beau seemed to be more than holding his own and Zoe didn't want to end the conversation until he had been fully refuted. Gillian spoke up, choosing to ignore Adrienne's suggestion.

"It all comes down to perspective," she said. She waved at Beau, her bracelets clacking. "The difference between us is that I don't see any country's military as a positive force. They're really vestiges of a past we can't leave fast enough behind us. Those warriors I was talking about. They need to become lovers. I think the world would be safer, and saner, place without any nuclear weapons, without any armies, without the US Army."

"With all due respect," Beau said coolly. "You and your husband would be speaking German tonight if it weren't for the US Army. All of Europe would. I'd call that positive, however vestigial."

"No one is questioning that," Levi Garber said, now wary, eager to smooth over the disagreement. "The military follows the policy set by our civilian leaders."

"But it's all part and parcel of the military-industrial complex," Zoe said. "I don't think our politicians really have much say so. They have to listen to Lockheed and Boeing before they listen to us. That's where the problem begins. The Army is part of the problem, not part of the solution."

"They'd still own blacks in the South if it weren't for the Army," Beau said. "It's times like that when everyone sitting safe in their comfortable living rooms fall over themselves in gratitude for the warriors. Warriors like Sherman and Phil Sheridan, who brought the fear of God to the South. Sheridan rolled right through the Shenandoah Valley, burning everything in sight. When a local fired on them, and they captured him, Sheridan's troopers strung 'em up from the nearest tree. Sheridan and his men understood what they were fighting for. They thought slavery was evil, and they didn't think negotiating was going to make it go away."

The room fell silent. They shared an embarrassment, Adrienne could see, at Beau's outburst. Derek had fixed his gaze over Beau's head, avoiding eye contact. Levi and Zoe Garber sat in awkward, stunned silence. Gillian, strangely, didn't seem fazed in the least; a slight smile played at the corners of her mouth.

"If you'll please excuse me, Mrs. Garber," Beau said to Zoe, rising to his feet, towering over the table. "I'm going to step outside for some fresh air."

"I'll join you," Adrienne said and turned to the Garbers and their guests. "Please excuse me, too."

Adrienne led Beau through the kitchen which was outfitted with the latest appliances and with the same gleaming wood floor. From the living room they could hear a hushed conversation between Zoe Garber and her husband. The Hawthornes were silent.

Adrienne and Beau stepped out the back door onto an extensive redwood deck. She took a package of Camels from her sweater pocket and offered him a cigarette, her hands shaking slightly from the emotion. He shook his head. She went ahead and lit up, exhaling her first long drag into the night air. Beau leaned next to her on the railing of the deck.

"I shouldn't lose my temper like that," he said. "But I can only listen to that crap for so long. That comment about how historians would believe that we were responsible for the Cold War was just too much. If this country is so screwed up, what the hell is that Brit asshole doing living here?"

"Please keep your voice down, Beau," she said. "I don't think Derek would appreciate being called a 'Brit asshole.'"

"I don't believe he'd think any less of me. I'm sure he considers me as an ill-mannered Jack Tripper type. Ready to nuke the Evil Empire back to the Stone Age."

"They're coming from a different place."

"You can say that again," he said.

"Shush," she said. "Don't waste the energy."

"You're right."

"Phil Sheridan," she said. "Where the hell did that come from?"

"I don't know. A moment of crazed inspiration."

"Phil Sheridan." She shook her head, but she knew Beau could see her grinning in the dark. "I can't take you anywhere. I'd forgotten about your temper."

"I haven't," he said. "Forgot about my temper, that is. I wish I had better control of it. I'm overreacting, I know." He exhaled deeply. "I hope I haven't made things untenable for you with your friends."

"They're not my friends," she said. "They're Hugh's."

She didn't want to say anything more, but she knew that when she told Hugh about the evening he would be angry with her. Hugh despised public confrontations and he would blame her for having invited Beau to the Garbers. Hugh had met Beau once, and hadn't cared for him, and this night would more than justify his initial negative opinion.

"I'll apologize to them when we go back in," Beau said. "I just need a moment or two more here outside."

"Thank you," she said. "Part of me wishes you wouldn't apologize, but it will be awkward if you don't. For me."

"Hugh?"

"Yes, I'm afraid that he won't be pleased with me."

"I'm sorry."

"Once you've made your apologizes we should go," she said. "It'd be awkward to stay."

"I'm afraid I've ruined your evening," he said. "It's my fault. I should have kept my cool. I hate what we've come to, the conflict with the other side, more than they can know. I've seen the consequences. I hate talking about it. In there I just reacted reflexively to their smugness. I guess you can only take so much. You can see how it torques me off when I hear them attacking our motives."

"You just have to ignore it."

He paused, struggling with his emotions. "I wish I could take them up with me in a Cessna or a Beechcraft and head west. Fly across the country, under the cloud cover, and then have them look down and see what the landscape looks like from up there. The farmland and small towns with their baseball diamonds and water tanks and grain silos and railroad crossings and the vastness of it all."

"And then what?"

"I'd have them pick any place, any town, at random and we'd put down at the nearest airport and find the town center and start asking the locals why they think our military is still in Europe. Why we're still there forty years after the war. I know what we'd hear. They're not happy about us being there, but the last time we left we had to go back and at a terrible cost. There's certainly no territorial ambition. What would we want with Europe? Hell, look around. We don't need the rest of the world. We could be self-sufficient and close our borders and not miss a beat. So no one wants our people there, or in any other foreign place, a minute longer than necessary. I only wish the Garbers and the Hawthornes could hear it. Then they might understand."

He stopped, lost in his thoughts, his face a study in intensity. She recognized, and not for the first time that night, Beau's resemblance to another difficult man, his father, the Professor. They shared a rigidity, an unwillingness to compromise, on what they saw as matters of principle and neither could leave well enough alone; they seemed incapable of letting a challenge pass. She could imagine that, in his time, the Professor had roiled a comfortable Hodge Road dinner party or two with his blunt, direct opinions.

Looking at Beau, his arm brushing lightly against hers, she remembered the fierce desire she'd felt for him the summer they'd been lovers. She wished she had been older, closer to his age, more experienced, more aware. She might have found a way to keep him longer as a lover. The truth was that she was still attracted to him, she knew, despite herself, despite the intervening years. In fact she couldn't imagine a time when she wouldn't find Beau desirable.

She started to say something to him, but realized that, for the moment, Beau was lost to her. He was looking up from the deck at the constellations above. She studied him for a moment, wondering what he was thinking. Was he soaring above the wingless and the earth-bound, above all of those who, like her, could never understand what it might be to fly alone in the clear, clean dark night sky?

8

The Jugglers

"I will teach you, little one," Teresa promised Katie. "If that is what you want."

Katie nodded in reply, offering Teresa her most solemn face, her freckled brow furrowing in concentration. But it was also clear that she doubted Teresa.

"Teresa," she said. "Do you really know how to juggle?"

Teresa leaned over to brush Katie's bangs off her forehead, marveling at her long, delicate eyelashes. When Kate grew up, when she lost her little girl awkwardness, she would be a great beauty, Teresa decided. Men would pursue her.

She knew what Katie was thinking. How could Teresa know how to juggle? Teresa, so old and so foreign and so strange. How could it be? But at the same time, Katie wanted to believe that Teresa could teach her. For days on end her brother Teddy had been teasing Katie about his newly acquired ability to juggle, lording his achievement over her. She was desperate to end her older brother's monopoly of the skill, and with Teddy away at summer camp for a week, Katie saw her chance.

"I know how," Teresa replied. "You shouldn't doubt me, Katie."

"Who taught you?"

"My brother Raul. He taught me when I was a little girl. You see, my brother dreamed of working in the circus, so he became an excellent juggler."

"He juggled in the circus?"

"No, Raul became a soldier instead. That was after we came to California. And then, when he returned to us from being a soldier, he became a gardener."

Katie considered what Teresa had told her. Then she asked how old Teresa had been when she learned to juggle.

"Just about your age. I was ten or eleven years old. We moved from my family's village to California a few years later."

"Then I could learn," Katie said. "Teddy keeps saying that I'm too young. Please teach me."

"Get me those things he juggles with," Teresa said. Katie skipped away, eager to find the beanbags. They had been a gift to all of the Vanderveck children from their uncle Francis, the señora's younger brother. On the afternoon he gave them the present, Francis had taught Teddy to juggle. Since then, Teddy had hoarded the beanbags, jealously keeping them from Katie.

When Katie had first asked Teresa about juggling, the baby had been asleep for almost ten minutes. Teresa figured that she had at least an uninterrupted hour or so before Shannon awoke—enough time to show Katie her juggling. Then Teresa would prepare lunch for Katie, and hope that Shannon wasn't too cranky after finishing his nap. With any luck Teresa could start the laundry. Señora Vanderveck was due back from her errands in the city at one o'clock.

Teresa heard Katie cry out in triumph. She had located Teddy's hiding place for the beanbags, under the couch in the family room. Katie ran back with the bags, her braids dancing about her shoulders. She offered her newly-found treasure to Teresa with both hands.

"It's been many years since I have juggled," she told the child as she accepted the red, green, and yellow fabric bags. "*Juegos malabares*, we call it at home."

"Is that Spanish for juggling?"

"That's right," Teresa said. "But we juggle the same way. It doesn't matter if you are in Mexico, or in America, or in China, it's the same."

Teresa cradled the beanbags in her hands, surprised at the simple pleasure she felt at holding them. She placed two of the bags, the green and yellow, in her right hand and the remaining one, the red bag, in her left, gently cupping her fingers around it.

She gave Katie a wary smile and then started, lofting the green bag into the air. Next she launched the red one and saw, to her dismay, that her first toss had soared too high and wide of the mark. The green bag spun away, out of reach, and Teresa, distracted, missed the red bag as well.

Katie looked at the bags on the floor, and then back at Teresa, doubt and confusion etched on her young face. Teresa bent over to pick up the bags, hiding her embarrassment. She tried to remember the last time she had juggled. It must have been at one of Raul's birthday parties in Pomona, but that had been ten years ago, before his heart problems, before she moved north to Ventura to be closer to Luz and her husband and their babies.

"Let me try again," she said. "I just need to get used to it again."

It took her five minutes before she began to feel comfortable with the motions of juggling. Katie stood to the side, silently watching as Teresa fumbled with the beanbags. Then, gradually, Teresa found her rhythm and the bags started to flow in smooth crescents before her, cresting at eye level. Katie gasped when Teresa successfully juggled four times in a row.

Teresa then risked a glance at her. Katie's face was now adorned with a smile, her faith in her Teresa restored. Teresa handed the bags back to Katie with a flourish.

"You see, I can juggle," she said. "Tomorrow we will begin to learn together. Soon you will be a brilliant juggler."

Katie had finished lunch when Señora Vanderveck returned from shopping. As always, the señora looked like one of the poised fashion models in the magazines Teresa scanned at the beauty salon on Voluntario Street. The señora was thin and very pretty. Only if one looked closely did her age show in the skin around the mouth and eyes. She paid great attention to her make-up and hair and clothing, but Teresa didn't blame the señora for vanity. Teresa knew she was trying to please Mr. Vanderveck. It was *Mr.* Vanderveck, for he insisted Teresa call him that instead of "Señor."

Mr. Vanderveck could be very critical of the señora's appearance, of the way she or the children were dressed, or of how clean Teresa, and by extension the señora, kept the house. Once, in Teresa's presence, he made the señora return upstairs and change her outfit because he said the colors clashed with the señora's complexion. Teresa was embarrassed for the señora.

Yet Teresa had learned that you could not judge a marriage from the outside. She had also seen a warmer side to Mr. Vanderveck. He could be tender, and mindful of the señora's feelings. Who knew what went on between a man and a woman, what kept them together? Sometimes there was more going on when the couple fought, Teresa believed, than when they ignored each other. She and Manolo certainly had had their share of fights, and yet they had loved each other fiercely.

Katie ran to her mother to share her excitement, tugging at her sleeve in a bid for immediate attention.

"I saw her, Mom," Katie said. "It was so neat. Teresa can juggle."

"Can she, now?" the señora replied in her breathless voice, the voice that made her sound like an actress, the voice she used when she talked to her Montecito friends on the phone.

"Teresa said she would teach me," Katie said. "She learned when she was my age."

"That's very sweet of Teresa," the señora said.

"Can I start learning now?" Katie asked.

"Teresa won't be with us this afternoon," the señora said. "We're going downtown. But perhaps tomorrow, when Shannon is sleeping, Teresa can teach you." She turned to Teresa. "If that is all right with Teresa."

"That would be fine," said Teresa, and this time Katie ran to her and hugged her in delight.

When Teresa left a short while later, after hanging up the last of the laundry in the basement and vacuuming the living room, Katie followed her to the driveway.

Katie tugged at Teresa's hand. "Teresa," she said. "I didn't really doubt that you could juggle."

"You didn't?"

"Not really. If I hurt your feelings when I asked if you really knew how to juggle, I'm sorry."

"It's nothing," said Teresa. "*De nada.*"

"Forgive me?"

"I forgive you," Teresa said and Katie quickly kissed her on the cheek and then skipped away to the back porch. Teresa felt tears welling in her eyes, and she coughed sharply to mask her feelings.

Katie watched from the porch as Teresa drove away. In her rearview mirror Teresa saw the child waving to her and wondered, not for the first time, what would happen with Katie when she reached the bewildering teenage years. Would she and her mother battle, the way Teresa and Luz had? Would Señora Vanderveck lose the closeness with her daughter, the sense of ease and trust, that Teresa had lost? Teresa hoped not.

Teresa felt lucky that the señora employed her to help with Shannon and the housework. The Vandervecks paid well and the señora was considerate, if distracted at times. But she did not forget that the Vandervecks, and their children, lived on a different plane from her and from most of the families, Anglo or Mexican, in the city. They were sheltered, buffered from worries and cares. Until she worked for the señora, Teresa had never imagined five television sets in one house.

That night she dreamed of the past, of the village of her childhood, of San Marcos.

She wears her best and favorite dress, her confirmation dress, and her hair is long, so long that it cascades to her waist, and it is shiny with the sheen of coal that has been in the rain. Her brother Raul is there with her and he gives her that sweet, sad smile of his and hands her three oranges. It is time for you to juggle, Teresita, he tells her. Remember to take care, for the oranges will bruise if they fall.

Her parents have come to the front of their house so they can watch her juggle. Papa sits on the low fence, a cigar clamped in his mouth, serenely puffing, a pose as familiar to her as the dusty streets of the village. Mama stands next to him, her arms folded, eager to see her Teresa perform.

Teresa realizes she is being watched by someone else. Across the street, behind a fence, there is a figure, a young man. A wide-brimmed hat shields his face. Raul calls out to her to commence, and so she resolves to ignore this other spectator, this stranger. Raul has taught her to focus only on the objects she is to juggle, to block out all other distractions, especially at first, when she begins, before she has settled into a pattern. That is when there is the most risk of faltering.

She begins to juggle. Her movements are deft and sure, her hands flutter like a bird about to softly land, just as Raul had taught her, and the oranges fly skyward. Her parents applaud, and Raul calls out encouragement. She is happy and fearless, she lifts the oranges into faster and faster flight, sure that she can recover them before they career out of control.

She dares not glance over for more than a moment for fear of dropping the oranges. But when she does steal a glance, she sees the stranger has removed his hat, and she make out his face. It is Manolo, her Manolo, and he knows that she recognizes him because he nods in his serious way, just as he did the first day they met in Los Angeles at the wedding of her cousin. Then he extends his right hand towards her. In his hand is a bouquet of wild flowers, as colorful as the fields from which it was gathered, and she wants it, not only because the bouquet is lovely, but because it is a gift from Manolo. She cannot, though, because to take the flowers she must stop juggling.

When he realizes this, that she cannot stop, he slowly withdraws his hand. Sorrow settles upon his face, a look she knows only too well. She is caught between conflicting demands, wanting to meet both and knowing that she cannot.

She starts to cry, all the time keeping the oranges aloft, timing her tosses to sustain a three-way balance, somehow aware that something even worse than Manolo's sorrow can happen if she falters. It begins to rain and the raindrops mix with her tears and her eyesight blurs as her Manolo walks away.

When Teresa awoke the next morning she remembered the sadness of her dream. Her mouth had gone dry and she felt fatigued from her restless night, weighted down, and she had a brief moment of dizziness when she got up out of bed. She gargled with Listerine and then brushed her teeth.

The dream had disturbed her enough that she thought of phoning Luz and then decided against it. Luz didn't like it when Teresa talked about Manolo. "Don't dwell on Papa," she would tell Teresa. "It's not healthy." Teresa had reconciled herself to this brisk, impatient, almost impersonal, side of her daughter. It was one reason she didn't tell her about her loneliness, or of her pain at not seeing much of Luz and the girls.

So instead Teresa tried calling Raul before she left for work. She wanted to tell him about it, about seeing Mama, Papa, and Manolo, of returning to San Marcos, but her nephew Ernesto, the junior at UCLA, answered the phone and explained that his father was on vacation. Teresa made him promise that he would tell Raul to call her when he returned home.

The call slightly delayed her departure for the Vandervecks. She especially disliked arriving late and so she drove a little faster on her way to the Vandervecks.

She found Katie waiting for her at the door, eager for her lessons to start. But not until the señora's departure for aerobics class and the start of Shannon's nap could Teresa begin tutoring the child.

She had Katie take one of the beanbags and toss it across her body to about eye level and then catch it with the other hand. Teresa coached her to achieve the same height on each toss. Katie caught on quickly and, after seven or eight successful tosses, asked when she could start real juggling.

"You must not rush, little one," Teresa told her. "Learn it the right way."

"But I need to juggle with all three beanbags," she said. "Teddy will make fun of me if he sees I can only handle one."

"Forget what Teddy says," Teresa said sharply. "Forget Teddy and what he says to you. It is Katie who is learning. It is Katie who will be juggling."

Teresa let her experiment with two bags while she went to the laundry room. When Teresa returned, Katie had stopped playing with the bags.

"I need help," she said. "I can't do it with two."

Teresa showed her how to follow one bag with the other, always trying to toss the bag to the same spots. While Teresa made a lunch of peanut butter and grape jelly sandwiches and Campbell's vegetable soup, Katie tried tossing two bags into the air. She stood near Teresa in the kitchen, and whenever she missed her toss, the bags would slap onto the tile floor. She quickly became frustrated.

"I will learn to do this," she said to Teresa, close to tears. "If it takes me all summer."

"It won't take that long, little one," Teresa reassured her. "With luck and patience it will be much sooner."

"How soon?"

"You should be juggling in a week."

"A week is too long," she said. "Teddy learned it in a day."

Teresa smiled at her impatience. While Katie physically resembled the señora, sharing her mother's blonde hair and fair skin, she had a completely different personality. Katie shared none of her mother's reserve or caution. She could be impetuous, stubborn, and passionate; rarely did she stop to calculate the consequences of her actions. Teresa believed that Katie must take after her father, the señora's first husband, in this, a man the señora never talked about. Katie and Teddy were both from the señora's first marriage.

"You must trust me," she told Katie. "If I am to be your teacher. You will learn it."

"Okay," the child said with a disarming smile. "I'll trust you."

But Teresa was unable to continue their first lesson. Shannon awoke crying and insisted on being fed immediately, and then the señora returned. It was Wednesday, Teresa's early day, and so she had to promise Katie that they would resume their juggling lessons the next day.

Teresa slept soundly that night, with no dreams to disturb her, or at least none that she could remember when she awoke. She was sure that the Vanderveck girl would juggle that day.

But they made slower progress than Teresa had hoped for. When Teresa arrived, señora Vanderveck took her aside and explained that Katie had practiced all afternoon and would have continued after dinner had the señora not taken the beanbags from her.

"She's very wound up about this juggling," the señora said. "I don't think I've ever seen her so anxious."

"How did she do? When she practiced."

"I couldn't really tell."

When they began the lesson, Katie proudly showed Teresa her progress. She could easily toss and catch two balls from hand to hand, although she had a tendency to throw the balls too high. Teresa praised her and began explaining how they would add the third ball when she heard Shannon fussing in his room. Teresa left Katie to soothe Shannon back into sleep. When she returned to the family room Katie was waiting for her.

Teresa juggled a few times and then handed Katie the third bag. "Why don't you try?" she asked.

Katie was too excited and rushed her tosses and the bags tumbled to the floor. She tried again, but failed. She pouted in frustration, again on the verge of tears.

"I can do it with two bags," she said. "This third bag is stupid. Why is three so hard?"

"You are rushing."

"I thought I could do it now."

"You must learn it step-by-step," Teresa explained. "Think of Shannon. He must crawl before he walks."

Shannon's wailing interrupted their discussion. Teresa had just finished changing Shannon's diaper when she heard the kitchen door open and the señora calling out for her. She brought the baby with her to the kitchen. The señora announced that Katie could watch one of her favorite Winnie the Pooh videos, something she didn't normally allow during the week, and then drew Teresa aside.

"Do you want to encourage her to continue?" the señora asked after Katie was out of the room. "I'm afraid she will be disappointed."

"She is close to learning," she told the señora.

"Mr. Vanderveck and I talked last night and he thinks perhaps it's a mistake to push Katie on this."

"Push her? Who pushes her?"

"You're right," said the señora. "Forgive me. She's not being pushed, per se. I know this is something Katie wants to do, but my husband doesn't like how frustrated she gets. He expects peace and quiet when he comes home, and I can't blame him."

"One more day," Teresa said. "Let her try for one more day. If she doesn't get it by then, we will stop."

"One more day?" Teresa could see the señora was weighing whether it was worth risking her husband's disapproval. She paused, and Teresa knew then that she would relent. "I will let you try for one more day," she said. "But you must tell Katie that she should not practice tonight when her father comes home."

Teresa nodded, keeping her full opinion of the matter to herself. She had no doubt that the señora could sense her disagreement. Had it been solely Teresa's choice, she would let Katie keep trying until she got it. Teresa didn't see how any other decision made sense, but there was much about the way the Vandervecks lived that Teresa didn't understand.

On the drive home Teresa found herself growing sleepy. She felt strangely light-headed and dizzy when she reached her front door. Once inside, she sat down at the kitchen table to rest. After ten minutes she felt better and decided to take a nap.

Later that night her brother Raul called her from San Diego, where he was vacationing. She turned off her television show, the "Wheel of Fortune," which she watched most nights, so they could talk. She told him about teaching Katie to juggle, and about her dream. They agreed that it was strange that her Manolo had appeared in the dream, because he had never visited San Marcos.

"We kept saying that we would go," Teresa said. "But we never did."

"Ernesto wants to see the village," Raul said. "He's the only one of my kids who seems to care. I think it's this Chicano Studies course he is taking. He wants to get back to his roots. We'll see. He thinks of Mexico as *otro lado* now, not the other way around. Ernesto is an all-American boy, now. I can't imagine him living anywhere without a cable television hook-up."

That made her laugh. Raul always made her laugh. She thought about mentioning the idea of moving to Pomona. She knew she wouldn't be as lonely there, but Raul's health had not been the best, and she didn't want to be a burden in any way. So, instead, she got Raul to talk about his vacation and by the end of the call she felt comforted the way she had in the old days when she and Raul and Manolo had sat around and played cards and talked through any troubles.

That next morning she awoke with an upset stomach. She had no appetite for breakfast. She found herself praying that Katie would juggle before the day was out.

She felt no better on the drive to the Vandervecks. She stopped at a convenience store on the way and forced herself to drink a cup of coffee, light and sweet. The coffee warmed her stomach and soothed her, although she still felt short of breath.

When Teresa arrived at the Vandervecks, the Señora had to leave immediately. She did not have time to talk to Teresa, she explained, because she had a doubles match at the tennis club and wanted to get there early enough to warm up with her partner.

Teresa put Shannon in his high chair and aligned it towards the family room so he could watch her and Katie. She gave him a small bottle of juice and he sat with the bottle, content to suck on the nipple. Then she started Katie's lesson. She began by rebuilding the child's confidence, taking Katie through the earlier stages that she had mastered. She had Katie toss and catch one bag, and then two bags, and then slowly had her try the exchange.

Then once Katie seemed comfortable, Teresa made her stop, and sit next to her.

"You must relax," she explained. "Today we cannot rush."

"I want to do this so much," Katie said. "That's why I rush."

"You must not be so serious, little one," said Teresa. "It should be fun."

On the drive over to the Vandervecks she had tried imagining what the world looked like through Katie's eyes, but found she could not. Her own upbringing in San Marcos had been so different. It was difficult, if not impossible, for Teresa to relate her childhood even to that of Luz's daughters, Maribel and Sandra, let alone Katie Vanderveck.

"I want it to be fun," said Katie, "but I get angry when I can't do it."

Teresa thought for a moment. "Please watch me," she said. "Watch me very closely."

Teresa juggled the bags as slowly as she could while still keeping them in the air. "Now close your eyes and imagine in your mind what you saw," she said. "Then imagine yourself juggling the balls. Picture it in your mind."

She handed the beanbags to Katie. "I want you to smile, first, before you begin. And also take a deep breath. In and out."

"Okay," Katie said, offering Teresa a grimace so contrived that both of them laughed.

"That's better," said Teresa. "It's easier to juggle when you are laughing. I'm going to put Shannon down for his nap. You start without me."

When she returned, Katie gave her a quick smile. "I almost got it," she said. "Almost."

She began tossing the bean bags, and then, before she had time to think, completed a full juggle. Startled by her success, Katie dropped the bags. "I did it!" she said, breathless in her excitement.

"That you did. Try again, and this time relax. Remember, nice and easy."

Katie juggled twice and then lost her concentration. It took her three or four more tries before she was able to sustain a full juggle. Then she managed to juggle three times, and then five times and her confidence grew.

They practiced together for more than a half hour. When Shannon awoke, Teresa told Katie that it was getting close to the time that her mother would return. Katie kept interrupting her practice to run to the kitchen window to see if she could spot the señora's Mercedes.

So eager was Katie for her mother to see her juggle that when the señora did arrive, Katie didn't want her to take a shower and to change, which was the señora's routine when she came home from playing tennis at the club.

The señora sat on the family couch, her pleated tennis skirt spread out in a semi-circle. Katie took a deep breath, as Teresa had coached her. She began juggling and completed ten iterations before she stopped, letting all three bags land in her hands.

"That's incredible," the señora said. "Katie, you are juggling by yourself."

"I know, Mommy."

Tears came to Teresa's eyes. She glanced over and could see the señora had been moved as well. At that moment Teresa felt a closeness to the señora, and she found herself hoping that in the years to come the señora would make more of connection with Katie than Teresa had with her daughter.

"That's wonderful," the señora said. "You must show your father when he comes home."

"Sure," said Katie. "But I really wanted you to see it first."

Later, after Teresa had finished washing and drying the lunch dishes and was ready to go, Señora Vanderveck took her aside. She handed Teresa the envelope with her weekly salary in cash.

"You have done marvelous work," she said. "I don't think I've ever seen Katie so excited."

"Thank you," Teresa said. "It was my pleasure." She feared, needlessly as it turned out, that the señora might try to pay her more, and she didn't want that. Teaching Katie to juggle had been her gift to the child.

Katie followed her to her car again. "Thank you, Teresa," she said.

"Now you can show Teddy."

"I suppose so."

"Don't you want him to see that you can juggle?" Teresa could sense that Katie was troubled by something.

"I do. But when he comes back I won't have as much time with you. I liked it when it was just you and me. And Shannon, but he sleeps most of the time."

Katie hugged her again, before Teresa could respond, and then fled to the house.

Teresa was surprised how tired she felt on the way home to the Eastside. She was bone weary: it reminded her of when she first came to Ventura and spent her days on her hands and knees scrubbing bathroom floors in homes and hotels.

She ate a small taco for dinner and treated herself to a beer, in celebration, which she usually didn't do because it roiled her stomach and gave her gas. She took some Pepto-Bismol after dinner, grimacing at the chalky, too-sweet taste, and watched half of "Wheel of Fortune" until, exhausted, she decided to go to bed.

That night she dreams again.

She is back in the village, lying in her parents' bed, with the window open. She feels old and weak, without the strength to rise from the bed, although she doesn't really want to, because she is so comfortable. It is late afternoon, the cool of the evening lies just ahead, and the last of the day's sun spreads light in dappled patterns across the bedspread. There are freshly cut wildflowers in the vase on the bedside table.

She looks over to the window and discovers Katie there, standing just outside the window. Raul is next to her and the two of them smile at her, sad-sweet smiles. There is something comforting about them standing there. It reminds her of the last scene in The Wizard of Oz, a film from Teresa's childhood, when Dorothy awakens from her dream journey and finds herself at home at the farm in Kansas and with all her friends around her bedside.

Why are you here? she asks them, and Katie responds in her little-girl voice that they have come to juggle for her. Isn't that what you wanted? Isn't that why you taught me?

Why are we in San Marcos? she asks Raul.

Raul looks at her tenderly and tells her in Spanish not to confuse her pupil, and he motions towards Katie and so Teresa stops asking questions.

Raul moves into his juggler's stance and they both begin to juggle, all at once, six crystal globes lofted into space. Their hands speed the transparent balls into flight without hesitation, a flow of movement and light as the glass reflects the waning sun.

Teresa gasps, mesmerized by the intervals of rising and falling, as the crystal balls dance in the air. She strains to follow their full trajectory as they spin up into the sky. The choreography is so fluid, so seductive, that, try as she might, she finds that she cannot take her eyes from the juggling.

She sighs. The sparkling spheres are so striking against the distant mountains and the sky beyond, the sky across which the stars themselves circle through the universe. She feels a touch on her left shoulder, a gentle touch of a hand, and without turning she knows it is Manolo. He is standing, silently, by her bedside.

She places her hand over his, all the while watching the juggling, and just as gently, he withdraws his hand. There is nothing else now, just her and the crystals, looping and swirling in an infinite dance, defying gravity, and then the sudden, hushed, final arrival of the night, and then all is dark and silent.

9

Daylight

I'm a girl who loves daylight. My favorite part of the day has always been the first hours after dawn, when the sun begins to illuminate the world around us.

I can't stand Daylight Savings Time—they ought to call it Daylight Losing Time, because in December and January and February it means in much of the country that it gets dark before five o'clock.

Florida is wonderful for daylight. It's closer to the equator so the sun sets later, even during the winter.

As you might imagine, wherever I live, I'm up at first light. Daylight is too precious to be wasted.

I'm a Marine brat. My childhood featured interrupted friendships and sudden uprootings, multiple schools, and moving vans. At least once we hadn't unpacked all of our belongings from the cardboard boxes before we were off again to a new Marine base in a new godforsaken location. That explains a lot, doesn't it? It helps explain why I crave stability, why I long for a spot to call home. But, at the same time, it also explains why I'm restless, and why I haven't stayed in one place for too long. I've grown accustomed to starting over, to bailing out of the old locale and moving on to new digs. Fresh starts. Clean slates.

Now I can't remember names or faces that well, which is probably a function of rootlessness, of moving around so much. Your mind can absorb and retain only so much. I'm lousy about most dates, too. I'm fuzzy about when exactly I graduated from high school, officially, since we were in transit between one of Daddy's postings and I missed out on the formal graduation ceremonies.

I don't have early Alzheimer's. I do recall Drew's birthday, September 19, 1982, but the birth of your only child is something no Mom is ever going to forget. He arrived at 6:17 AM in birthing room Number Two in Mount Carmel West hospital in Columbus.

I'm better about places. I have a keener memory for them: cheap apartments and fancy hotel rooms, bedrooms and parlors, bungalows and split-levels, courtyards and gardens. I'm a whiz, comparatively speaking, at remembering places. I think that it is because they're concrete, real, definable. They're solid, an anchor of sorts for my memories. It's a bit strange that I can picture the cheap dresser and twin beds in the room my sister and I shared when I was in tenth grade but I can't, for the life of me, conjure up the face of the geometry teacher, Mr. Dickens, who saddled me with a "D" for my mathematical failings that year.

It just proves that the mind works in strange ways, or at least my mind does.

I've lived all over the country, north and south, east and west. I spent the summer that I turned nineteen living in Hart Crane's cottage in North Truro, near the tip of Cape Cod. I call it Hart Crane's cottage because the locals claimed that the poet (someone I'll confess I had never heard of before that summer) had stayed there back in the 1920s. By the time I summered there the cottage was the property of my then lover. He was a man with long, graceful hands and a knack for making money. He owned the Hart Crane cottage, of whose literary heritage he was very proud. He also owned an apartment on the Upper East Side in New York, and a condo in Aspen. I never made it to the Aspen condo, which I regret, because I've heard the skiing shouldn't be missed.

He spent that summer trying, desperately, to keep me intrigued. He was twenty years older than me and the gap in our ages made him insecure. Once, on a romantic whim, he chartered a private plane and flew us to Bar Harbor on Deseret Island in Maine for lunch. We had boiled whole lobsters and fresh corn. We were back at the Provincetown Airport before dark. Twice we drove to Boston and stayed at the Ritz-Carlton on Commonwealth Avenue near the Public Gardens. We made love there in a king-size bed whose sheets bore the scent of French perfume. We visited the Isabel Stuart Gardner Museum and the Museum of Fine Arts and then went shopping in the trendy clothing boutiques on Newberry Street, where he spent thousand on me for two outfits and matching shoes.

We both knew that he would fail, that we wouldn't last. I was too young and he needed control I would never give. But I've learned that there are times when you play out the hand even when the cards are bad, and this was one of those times. It seemed the right thing to do, to give him his chance. If you asked him today, I don't think, even in hindsight, that he would complain. He delighted in lavishing money and attention on me, in being the first to introduce me to new experiences. I represented a welcome distraction from the deals he was always negotiating on the phone with investment bankers in New York and London.

I can't remember his face clearly now. I can picture his Cape Cod cottage. It had four rooms: a kitchen, two bedrooms, and a living room. He was a tidy man. He kept it painstakingly clean and neat. I remember the aroma of lemon cleaner and sea air; it lacked the musty cramped smell of many summer homes.

I distinctly recall that the cottage had an outdoor shower. Strangely enough, it was that shower which first exposed his neediness. The water cascaded onto a smooth concrete slab from a shiny shower head angled away from the house. You operated the shower by pulling down on a chain. The water was warm, passing through the water heater in the small basement of the cottage. The shower area was screened from view by the cottage on one side and a small wooden privacy panel on the other. A copse of pine trees to the west partially blocked the view of the bay. After swimming I'd strip off my bathing suit and shower there, goose bumps often dotting my arms and legs from the breeze. Blissfully naked. I'd towel dry and, with a towel wrapped around me, go inside to change.

The first time he discovered me there showering in the buff, he became visibly upset. I had a great body then, and I was proud of it in the way you are when you're younger and don't realize that it won't last forever. I didn't understand why he was so disturbed, but I figured it was some variation on the jealous older lover trip he seemed to take now and then. He insisted that I shower with my bathing suit on and became quite angry when I laughed at him. He finally calmed down and I thought nothing more of it.

The second incident came a few days later, when he again found me showering in the nude. He began yelling at me, ugly things, and when I yelled back he stopped. He realized that he had overstepped. He tried to explain. He claimed that he didn't want the neighbors to see me, which was absurd, because the shower was hidden from view and the nearest house was quite a distance. (And so what if they did? I didn't have anything to hide.) I told him that. In response he said the strangest thing to me: "You are a cruel and wanton girl, Liza."

I couldn't accept that he was trying to tell me how to live, how to act. You can't give in to that, not even once. I think that like most wealthy men, what he really wanted wasn't intimacy and love but possession and control.

"When you are ready to settle down," he told me once, at the end, when it was clear that we were finished, "call me. It won't matter to me who you have been with, or where you have been. Please just call me."

He did know how to flatter, I will grant him that. It is no small quality in a man.

Later I went to the library to read Hart Crane's poetry. He didn't write much, he had one of those tragic, artistic deaths before his time. The truth is that I didn't really care for his poems. His language seemed cold and artificial. I remember one lyrical phrase, though, that I particularly liked, in his poem "The Bridge," when he wrote about New York harbor at dawn. It was how a star "as though to join us at some distant hill, turns in the waking west and goes to sleep."

Then there was my stretch in California, when my college roommate Jill Sturm and I scraped up the rent for an A-frame with stained-dark wood on the edge of the Napa Valley. The house made me think of an Indian teepee, with its triangular shape and steeply pitched roof. This came a few years after my summer on the Cape. I had made my way west after a stop in New York City and two years in Austin, Texas. Jill had called me in Texas and asked me to come share the house with her. I couldn't see a reason not to, and so I packed up and went.

Jill kept her hair close-cropped then, and she liked wearing blue jeans, Levi's shirts, leather vests and hiking boots. I'm sure our neighbors pegged her as a lesbian—which she wasn't—and figured I was too, (the feminine half of the equation). But no one really cared, and we were left alone.

The house had generous open spaces. It smelled of fresh-cut wood and smoke from the fireplace we used on chilly nights. Jill and I agreed there was no need for furniture to clutter the place up, so we slept on futons and when we had a party, which was almost every weekend, everyone sat around the living room on pillows. We didn't want to spare the money for furniture anyway. We paid the rent by waitressing over in St. Helena at a breakfast and lunch place and finding odd jobs, like house-sitting for a rich couple for a month. There wasn't much money left over.

I paid little attention to the passage of time then, and the days slipped seamlessly by. I didn't think twice about it, the way you do when you're younger and don't fully appreciate that you only have so many days allotted, so much time on the clock.

"Everyone seems so mellow here," I told Jill after a few months. "So mellow. It's one of those clichés that's true."

"I love the sound of that word," she said. "Mellow."

"You're much mellower yourself these days," I told her.

"I am? Then I hope it rubs off on you, love," she said. "You could use more mellowness in your life. Mellow yellow."

From that point on, whenever I said the word, Jill would crack up.

But that very mellowness made me restless. I didn't want to take tai chi lessons with the ancient Cantonese woman Jill had discovered in Santa Rosa. I was bored with smoking dope in somebody's hot tub at midnight and enthusing about the way the stars filled the night sky.

So I took up with a boy who wanted to be a Formula One race-car driver. Looking for adventure, like the song says, heading out on the freeway. Scott was slight in build and handsome in an odd, almost elfin way: he had long eyelashes, delicate features, and a shy way of avoiding eye contact. His pride and joy was his green Porche, a 911 model. I'd go with him when he raced through the wine country's winding, two-lane roads and when he tested his skill along the twisted curves of the coastal highway. He would put the top down and the wind would whip past us as he floored it, pushing the car well past ninety miles per hour in the straightaways, and sliding into turns at high speeds.

It was reckless. There were times I closed my eye. But he was completely alive and I was drawn to that quality. Now I know how stupid it was. Half of the stupid, dangerous things men do are to impress women, the other half they think up themselves.

I think I was also intrigued by Scott because he didn't fall hard for me. It wasn't romantic gamesmanship on his part. He wasn't trying to ensnare me. He just had other interests. I ranked a distant second to the rush he got with speed and I saw that as a challenge. When we made love, no matter how far our passion would take us, I somehow felt that we couldn't ever match the thrill for him of that damn car.

Eventually he left me to go to San Diego, to try to catch on as a driver at a race track down there. He didn't ask me to tag along. By then, I wasn't as intrigued. I had begun to fear riding in his car, sharing the stupid risks he took. I figured at some point Scott would wrap that 911 around a tree, and I didn't want to be there.

After Scott left, I didn't see much of a reason to stay. I had already tired of the whole Napa scene: the aging hippies in tie-dyed shirts who drove around the valley in their VW buses, the hand-to-mouth artists, the gay couples escaping San Francisco, the tourists on wine-tasting tours, the rich retirees building their million dollar castles. I missed the tension and conflict of city living. I think I missed the urban hostility (that's right, the hostility.)

When I told Jill I wanted to move on, she wasn't surprised.

"I didn't think you would stay," she said.

"You didn't?"

"You're too jumpy, Liza. There's not enough going on here. I don't think you're ready for that yet. You're not willing to become mellow yellow."

I didn't want to argue. We would always be friends, no matter where we ended up. She always spoke her mind.

"You're probably right," I told her. "I'm not ready."

"You would have stayed longer if we were living in San Francisco," she said wistfully.

I offered to hang around until she could find another room-mate, but she told me not to wait.

"I just want you to be happy," she said. "You need to keep looking."

The smallest space I ever lived in was a one-room apartment on East 23rd Street in Manhattan. Sub-leased from an aspiring actress who was living out in L.A. I stayed by myself in that walk-up, the year that my Daddy died. The apartment had a tiny stove and a ludicrously narrow bathroom. I think only six inches separated the shower curtain from the edge of the toilet. The wallpaper in the apartment was a ghastly abstract pattern that might have looked cool for about fifteen minutes in 1976.

I didn't really care. I was oblivious to both the decor and any missing creature comforts. I was so out of control that year, but I kept telling myself, so what? I did more than my share of cocaine—blow, we called it then. I did more than my share of men, all ages, colors, sizes, shapes. I stayed stoned a lot of the time.

Looking back now, I wonder how I made it through that time, physically and emotionally. I have fragmentary Manhattan memories. I wore a sarong dress that summer with Swedish clogs. In the fall, I cut myself badly with a serrated knife on the palm of my hand and ended up with six stitches, sown up by a nervous Pakistani intern at New York University Hospital's emergency room. That winter I went cross-country skiing with one of my friends through Central Park after a particularly heavy snow. I also discovered the great taste of Ron del Barrilito rum, distilled in Bayamon, Puerto Rico. And I learned of my Daddy's death in a phone call from my Mom on an April Sunday morning.

The funeral remains a blur in my memory. I wore sunglasses the entire time, in the church and at home, and I was flying anyway with a little help from my pharmacological friends. My Mom flew back to New York with me. She just shook her head when she saw my sublet. She slept on my bed and I unrolled a sleeping bag and spent the week on the floor.

Mainly we walked, all over the city. She talked a lot about Daddy and their years together and how she didn't regret much. I only heard about half of it, because I was having a hard time concentrating.

"When did you know that Daddy was the one?" I asked her.

"The one?"

"The one you loved, the one you wanted to marry."

"It didn't happen that way," she said. "I married him because it seemed the right thing to do. Besides, I was pregnant with your older sister at the time."

"How come you didn't have any more kids after me?" I asked her. "Didn't Daddy want a boy, a son?"

"Of course. No matter what they say, all men want a son," she said. "But I couldn't have any more babies after you. You were a hard pregnancy, and I had to have a C-section. Afterwards the doctor told me I should have my tubes tied, because if there was a next time around, I could die. So that's what we did."

"I didn't know that," I managed to say. "You always just said that two was enough."

"It's not really the sort of thing you share with a teenager."

"What else don't I know?" I asked.

"Whatever you don't know, you shouldn't know," she said. "Don't look so hurt. You'll understand some day. Your Daddy wasn't a saint. But neither was I. A lot of being married is learning to work around that fact. Not to get stuck on it. I hope you remember that when you get married."

"I'm not getting married," I said. "I don't have the time."

I was wrong about that. I was hitched within two years, and Alan and I had Drew a year later. And my Mom's marital advice, like most of her advice, proved to be lousy.

The longest stretch I've lived in one place was in Florida, in a sleepy retirement town on the West Coast called Punta Blanca. Don't feel bad if you don't recognize the name, because Punta Blanca is halfway to the middle of nowhere. Drew and I followed my older sister Lauren there, after Alan and I separated.

Our house in Punta Blanca was one story with pink stucco, a green tile roof and a lime green interior—what were called Miami Vice colors at the time. We had a small lanai covering a leaky swimming pool in the backyard. Technically it was waterfront property, given that the property backed onto a canal which eventually connected to the harbor, but you couldn't get from our yard to real water in anything larger than a dinghy because a bunch of bridges blocked the way. But I liked it there. It was peaceful, a good place to raise a kid, and after my time in Pensacola I was prepared for the summer heat when it came.

Punta Blanca proved to be a very strange little town. There were still a few native Floridians, ranchers and shrimpers and small businessmen around, but the vast majority of its residents were newcomers, mostly retirees from the Midwest, amazed that they had escaped the bad weather and grateful for the near-tropical warmth. I never met so many nurses and physical therapists and hospital and nursing home workers. They were Lauren's friends. She'd started as a night nurse at one of the hospitals and worked her way into day shifts.

I had second thoughts about the move, almost immediately. I can't believe that we actually stayed six years there. But I wanted to get Drew through high school in one location (that's something I never had) and we did. It was harder to find a teaching job than I had thought. I began substituting at the high school, which I hated, because the students were often disrespectful or sullen or hostile. Drew hated it when I taught there and I don't blame him.

Alan had accused me of selfishness in moving to Florida. He believed that staying in Ohio, near him, would have been the best thing for Drew.

"You have the right to move there," he told me. "But it means I won't be seeing Drew more than once a year. If that."

"That's a choice you already made," I responded. "About what mattered to you."

"Ah, Liza. Don't be so damn hard on me. I've got enough guilt without this."

"I'm sorry," I told him. "I can't put my life in a holding pattern for you. Drew can't either. I wish it wasn't this way, either."

"You're the one moving."

"You're the one who left," I countered. "You're the one with things to work out."

"That's a fact," he said. "I'm not disputing that."

"I'm doing what I think I have to," I said.

"If this is what you have to do," Alan said, conceding. "If this is going to be best for you and Drew, I can't really fight it."

But I hated Alan for agreeing, and for the mess we had made of my marriage. It served me right for marrying a ladies' man. Despite my brave words, I was worried about Drew. After the move from Ohio, he withdrew into himself. It scared me, because we had always been such good friends. I had been teaching long enough to know how hard and dangerous the teen years could be and I didn't want to lose him.

Somehow we found a way. It wasn't easy. There were times when I found it hard to believe that this six-foot tall sullen teenager before me had once been a red-cheeked little boy who loved singing along to the Winnie-the-Pooh song: "willy, nilly, silly old bear." (Such images would always flash through my mind when we were in the middle of a heated argument over what he was old enough to do by himself.) I held onto that. It helped.

I felt like someone had pushed the pause button on the videotape of my personal life for those years. The same image, frozen in place, of dealing with whatever we had to. I was lonely at times. There wasn't any room there for a steady man. I was living in a small town where there were no secrets. None. I managed two longer vacations by myself during our time in Punta Blanca. Drew stayed with Lauren and I went down to Key West once and to Mexico, to Cancun, on another occasion. I pretended I could be a free spirit. And I faked it fairly well, but not for long.

The strangest spot I ever stayed in had to be the Monastery of Christ of the Mountains. It's about eighty miles north of Santa Fe, ten miles up a dirt and gravel road into the mountains, almost 6,500 feet above sea level. I spent two weeks there and I never really felt like I caught my breath there. The air was so thin and cold. My room was heated by a wood-burning stove (we split the wood as part of our work commitment) and it was lit by a kerosene lamp (only the refectory and chapel had electricity).

The room was small and incredibly Spartan: a bed with comforter, night table with wash pan and one saving feature, a small window in the adobe wall providing a stunning view of the mountains.

Jill had persuaded me to go, to make a retreat there. I fought her for two months over the phone long-distance before I agreed to go. I didn't think it made much sense for me. I have no use for organized religion. I didn't understand why Jill would think a Benedictine monastery would be a good place to sort out my thoughts, although I knew I needed to get away.

"This is the late nineteen eighties," I had reminded her. "You're suggesting that I go to a monastery? A Catholic monastery? Aren't Zen Buddhist temples the place to go now?"

"This experience will work for you," she told me. "It's in the mountains and there are no distractions. You hardly talk, because the monks observe the code of silence."

"How long were you there?" I asked her.

"I stayed a week after my brother died. I went up there depressed as hell, but I came back with the anger gone. It just seemed to float away."

"What do I do if I get there and it's a drag?"

"You leave," she said. "But that won't happen."

I was between boyfriends and tired of teaching, happy to have Drew off to college and ready for a change. I felt like I was burnt out. (That was the phrase we all used then).

It is amazing what you begin thinking about when you're stuck in the middle of nowhere (the *real* middle of nowhere) and there's only stark, white-washed walls inside to look at and breath-taking, but unchanging, scenery outside. Brother Nicholas told me over the phone that it took two or three days to leave the cares and concerns of the outside world behind. He was right. I didn't slow down and accept the pace of the monastery, the routine of prayer and work and common meal and reflection and sleep, for several days.

I found Brother Nicholas an intriguing man. He had been a physicist at Sandia, the nuclear weapons lab near Albuquerque, when he felt called to enter the monastic life. He was really the only monk a guest could talk to—the rest were observing their vows of silence.

It's also amazing what time and solitude bring to the surface. At first I slept fitfully, with dreams of Drew and my folks and even Alan interrupting my sleep. It got better after I tried meditating, closing my eyes and imagining the sweeter times in my past.

Certainly some of the things I regret surfaced. I don't have a lot to regret, though I have had my moments. I remember the time in high school when Daddy came up to New Orleans to get me out of a jam. I'd cut classes to drive up from Pensacola with one of my loser boyfriends, Lennie, and we'd gotten drunk on Bourbon Street and Lennie got in a fight with some redneck who was ogling my halter top and short shorts and we ended up in jail. Daddy came and bailed us out and once we were outside Daddy grabbed Lennie's shirt front and held him up against the truck and told him that if anything like this ever happened again Lennie would want to stay in jail rather than face Daddy. It worked, I guess, because Lennie disappeared from my life in a hurry. I feel bad about the pain it must have caused Daddy, the embarrassment, too.

I didn't look to lay the blame off on anyone else for the wrong turns along the way. What's the point of that? Sure, I wish Daddy had left the Corps and we'd settled someplace for keeps, and that Alan had kept his hands off other women, and that I hadn't wandered through most of my twenties. But there's no going back. No time machine to fix what was and shouldn't have been. I did cry a few times, thinking back, considering the pain.

I'll admit that my stay with the gentle brotherhood worked. I felt cleansed. I felt rested when I left Christ of the Mountains. I had energy. I told Brother Nicholas on my last day there that I would be coming back in ten years for another private retreat. He laughed when I told him I only had the patience for it once a decade.

I returned from New Mexico with a goal, of sorts: to find the right longitude and latitude and settle down at their point of intersection. I've never had much of a plan for my life. Perhaps it's the first signs of middle age, or maybe I'm tired of relying on chance or luck in finding my way, but I'm looking for a place now. I've drawn up the specifications. No more than an hour's drive to the ocean. Why that? I want to live near the water. We all need our fair share of negative ions, which is what surf and waterfalls offer in profusion. And I feel closed in, constricted, trapped, even, if I can't see the water.

My hometown is going to be near a University, because I like all the bookstores and coffee shops and tai chi lessons (the lessons I will probably never take), and strange hangers-on clustered around a college.

I cherish the change of seasons, so wherever I settle must have a distinct summer, fall, winter and spring. I need to see leaves, snow, ice, mud, the spring flowers and budding trees. It's strange, but I find the first snow of the season comforting.

There has to be an element of natural beauty. I've become selfish about that. I don't ever want to live in a hard-scrabble or tired place, where the houses are crammed together or there's no pattern to the town. I don't want to live anyplace where there are a lot of poor people. That sounds horrible, I know, but it's because I've been poor and I've lived in cold, inhospitable tired-out places with too many empty storefronts and parking lots with broken glass and too few trees. I don't want that.

I want neighbors who are friendly, but not nosy. Most of them should be relatively stable and in touch with reality. That excludes a lot of California. They can be religious as long as they don't get in your face and want to know about your personal relationship with Jesus Christ. There has to be a sense of tradition. That rules out all of the Sunbelt. I'd like a majority of the people there to be locals: to have spent most of their lives there. Public manners must be appreciated (so scratch New York, New Jersey, and most of New England from the list).

I've got the Rand McNally road atlas sitting on my dining room table and many nights, after I've cleared the table, I pour myself a glass of chilled white wine and leaf through the maps. I've narrowed the list to a dozen or so towns and cities, most of them in Virginia, North Carolina, and Maryland. I don't tell anyone which places, because I think that would be bad luck somehow. I'm being cautious about this, because I want to make a commitment.

And, of course, there's the daylight. It's a non-starter if leafy trees or tall buildings block the sun. I need the light, clear and strong. I want as much daylight as I can get. And I won't waste it. That's a promise.

10

Keepers

They anchored in a rolling surf on the Gulf of Mexico side of Cayo Costa, near the island's midpoint. Lars had maneuvered the *Valhalla* within twenty yards of the beach, just south of where two Australian pines uprooted by a storm now lay toppled, their branches extending into the water. He anchored the boat there, well within easy casting distance of the shallows and a line of small breakers. They were close enough to hear the sound of the waves slapping onto the narrow beach.

That long stretch of sand, crowded by the mangrove fringe of the barrier island, stood empty, clear of interlopers. Ben scanned the Gulf's waters to the north and to the south along the coastline. A few seagulls wheeled in flight over the surface of the water; no signs of boaters.

It would look like this after the Rapture, Ben thought. *Deserted*. His Baptist friends back in Bedford were convinced that when God gathered his saints to heaven at the end of time, as promised in the Book of Revelation, then the world would be emptied of the righteous. It would be as desolate and beautiful as when Hernando de Soto and the Spaniards, a band of sinners if there ever was one, arrived off Cayo Costa in the seventeenth century, intent on conquest and subjugation.

Their isolation pleased Lars. He preferred to fish alone, resenting competition whether from curious day-trippers or other guides, and he remained fiercely protective of what he regarded as his personal fishing spots. As a boy growing up in rural Indiana, Ben had seen how the territorial imperative took over whenever men hunted or fished, and so Lars' possessiveness seemed natural.

"This can be a good place to fish," Lars told them as he surveyed the area. "But I don't want to jinx us. Let's see what luck we have."

"Have you been here recently?" Thomas asked.

"A week ago, and the tide was running the same. Surf wasn't quite as rough. We found a lot of snook here."

"That sounds promising," Thomas said.

"You never know. Lots of variables. That's what makes it interesting. They should be here, but that's just me wishing out loud. My mother used to say that if wishes came true we'd all have candy and nuts for Christmas."

"I'll settle for catching some fish," Thomas said.

They cast to the edge of the beach, into the surf, using scaled sardines for bait. The *Valhalla*'s deck rolled with the incoming swells and Ben struggled to keep his footing; he could see that Thomas, a smaller man and usually more agile, faced the same problem of maintaining his balance. Thomas cursed softly. Lars stood by the console, effortlessly moving with the waves, and watched their struggle with unconcealed amusement.

Lars proved to be right about the attractiveness of the spot. Their first several casts attracted attention. The sardine on Ben's line had hardly vanished under the water when its frantic movement signaled a nearby predator, and then the line went taut with a strike. It proved to be a small snook, which surfaced twice, jumping in a vain effort to throw the hook. It took Ben three or four minutes to bring the fish to the boat.

"Nice work," Thomas said. "You take honors for first catch."

"Of course we can't keep this one," Lars said, as he deftly removed the hook and gently released the fish back into the Gulf. "Out of season, now. Get your bait back in the water, gentlemen, 'cause they're here."

Almost every cast produced another hit for Thomas or Ben. As they fought the snook to the boat's side, Lars encouraged them to keep constant pressure on the line so the fish couldn't break free. Once the leader had reached the tip of the rod, the fish was close enough to the boat for Lars to net. He'd quickly show them their catch, unhook the fish, and then release them back into the water by the stern of the boat.

Then, despite the rolling deck, Lars would move to the bait well and effortlessly re-bait their hooks so they could cast again. Ben was grateful for his help. He'd never been light on his feet; like many big men he'd learned to be cautious about relying on his sense of balance.

Ben paused and removed his polarized sunglasses; he wanted to see the true colors of one of the larger fish he had brought to the boat. After his eyes adjusted to the glare, Ben noted the snook's characteristic dark lateral line running the length of its body from the upper gill to the center of its forked tail. But this one had an unusual whitish hue to its skin, unlike the golden tone he was used to seeing.

"It looks like an albino," Lars said. "You find that sometimes this time of the year. The water here is so clear there's no coloration from silt."

"I've never seen that before," Ben said.

"You've got to get out more, then," Lars said.

"I keep telling Ben that," Thomas said . "He's too duty-bound."

"No more than you, Doctor Tom," Ben said. "It's the curse of our Bedford upbringing. You're supposed to feel guilty when you hunt or fish too often. It means you're neglecting work."

"Sometimes it needs neglecting. You should come down on vacation and visit more often. I'd be more than happy to drive over from Winter Haven to fish."

Lars interrupted to encourage them to start casting again. Ben found that if he let his baitfish swim against the tide, the natural motion would quickly attract a snook. A tug on his line would follow and the tip of the rod would bend towards the water as the fish tried to run from the sudden danger. Within twenty minutes Ben had caught six snook, and Thomas had brought three to the boat. Thomas also caught two reddish-hued mangrove snappers, which Lars put in the ice chest.

"You're on your way to dinner," Lars said, relaxing as he saw the day take form. There was always an edginess to Lars until his clients began catching fish; he took it as a personal affront, a challenge to his skill as a guide and his knowledge of the harbor, if the fishing was spotty.

"The snapper can be tomorrow's lunch," Thomas said. "Elaine promised she'd make us sandwiches if we could catch some fish."

For the past five summers Ben and Thomas had fished with Lars, scheduling a trip or two (and sometimes more when the fishing was especially good) whenever the Duncans vacationed in Florida. They had been fishing together since their childhood in Indiana. Thomas Stafford was Ben's oldest friend; they'd grown up together in Bedford and had roomed together all four years at I.U. They had stayed in touch through their years in graduate study and had been each other's best man.

It was a friendship that had grown and deepened over time. When Ben's mother and father had both died in one hellish six-month span in 1985, Thomas had flown north from Florida, both times, to be there. He'd stood by Ben's side through both funerals. Ben Jr. had stayed with the Staffords whenever he visited Florida and Darian Stafford, Thomas' oldest daughter, had lived with the Duncans in Bloomington when she took summer courses at I.U. For years Ben and Jill had visited the Staffords in Winter Haven after Thomas moved to Tampa for his residency in orthopedic surgery.

This summer Ben had reserved three weeks of vacation in August, with one week in Florida. His firm had added a new junior partner, a capable young woman recruited from the District Attorney's office, and Ben had gladly turned over several of his more pressing cases to her before he left.

Lars specialized in what the local guides called back bay, or back country, fishing: employing a shallow-draft skiff and light tackle to pursue gamefish like snook, redfish, and sea trout. Ben and Thomas had come to prefer it to other types of fishing. Years earlier, the two had chartered boats for tarpon fishing in Boca Grande Pass during the late spring and early summer, but had found the drift fishing involved too repetitive and slow-moving. They'd connected with Lars through Thomas' cousin, Kevin, who wintered on Boca Grande, and had used Lars as a guide.

Thomas took to Lars immediately. They shared a scientific bent, and Lars didn't mind answering Thomas' numerous questions about fishing techniques. It also helped that Lars always managed to find fish. He had the quiet self-confidence of a man who knew his craft. Thomas asked a lot of questions—about the tackle, the bait, the tactics chosen for different fish—and the answers just spurred more questions. Thomas wanted to get at the heart of the matter in all things. It was, Ben decided, a reflection of the intellectual hunger and attention to detail that, coupled with extraordinary hand-eye coordination, had made Thomas a great surgeon in his prime.

Lars also shared his stories about the Harbor, of sightings of Old Hitler, the legendary hammerhead shark reputed to patrol Boca Grande Pass, of the rumors that drug runners were responsible for the unsolved killing in 1979 of a fishing party of three—a guide and a honeymooning couple—in Turtle Bay. (They had been executed in cold-blood, their bodies discovered by a commercial fisherman. All three had been shot in the back of the head, kneeling on the foredeck of the fishing skiff.).

At Thomas' prompting, Lars also explained how the fishing in the area had changed over the years, of the rise and fall of the mulletmen and the shrimpers, of the free-spending sport fishermen and their high-stakes tarpon tournaments, of the recent introduction of saltwater fly fishing. "I've tried fly-fishing," Lars told them. "I guess I could attract more clients if I offered it. But it's too much damn work and it'd frustrate the hell out of first timers. You can't learn it in a day. I wore a suit and tie and worked in an office once. A salary slave. I know you don't want to come out on the water and be frustrated. You could just stay at work if that's what you wanted."

That was Lars—blunt, sometimes cranky, always plain-spoken and to the point. (Ben had noted the same bluntness in other guides and wondered whether the occupation attracted independent loners, or whether guides were expected to adopt the plain-speaking style, in the way stockbrokers he'd known always projected a bullish confidence and enthusiasm.) Lars had greeted them that morning with his signature directness when they boarded the *Valhalla* at the guide's dock near the Pink Elephant restaurant.

"What's our schedule for today?" Lars had asked "A full day of fishing?"

"We need to be back to the dock no later than five-fifteen or so," Thomas told him. "We're meeting our wives for dinner." They had parked on Bayou Avenue in the restaurant's parking lot.

"He's alerting you that we can't afford to be late," Ben said.

"I understand," Lars said, acknowledging him with a smile. "I was married once."

"So then you know the difference between a wife and a terrorist?" Thomas asked.

"Tell me."

"You can negotiate with a terrorist."

Lars liked the joke enough that he made Thomas repeat it; Ben figured Lars would recycle it with his next set of clients.

On the way to Cayo Costa they encountered a manatee in the harbor, its huge, brownish primeval body floating below them fifteen yards off their port side, the nicks and scars from props criss-crossing the animal's back. Lars had throttled back so they could see the animal, but Thomas hadn't launched his normal barrage of questions. Ben noted his friend's mood but didn't comment; most of the time when they fished Ben stayed quiet. He found it a relief not to have to talk, and he was content to let Thomas and Lars carry the bulk of the conversation.

As they fished off Cayo Costa's beach, Ben enjoyed the isolation of their morning anchorage. By choosing a Thursday for their trip, they avoided the heavier weekend boat traffic, and by fishing in August, the hottest month of the year, they were sure to encounter far fewer tourists. The scene appealed to Ben: the vastness of the Gulf at their backs, the sense of being left alone, of being able to focus solely on the task, the pleasurable task, at hand. Except for the occasional splash of a diving seagull or pelican, or the sounds of a distant airplane, it was quiet. Ben welcomed the warmth of the morning sun on his back and the breeze sweeping in from the west.

At one point later in the morning Ben looked over and saw Thomas' hands shaking slightly as he tried to adjust the drag on his reel. Lars had noticed as well: very little, if anything, occurred on the *Valhalla* that he missed. Ben contemplated the surgeon's predicament in late middle-age: your hands could betray you long before your wits or experience did. Lawyers were spared that embarrassment, yet a part of Ben envied Thomas, and Lars for that matter, for working with their hands, for the concreteness of their jobs.

Whether prompted by Thomas' difficulties, or by his sense that the fishing had slackened, Lars called to them to reel in their lines.

"We're about done here, I think," Lars said. "We'll get out of this chop."

"I won't complain," Thomas said, and Ben could see he didn't look well. Beads of sweat had gathered on his forehead, and a light, whitish foam had caked around the edges of his lips. His face had an ashen cast to it.

"Are you holding up all right?" Ben asked him.

"Touch of sea sickness," Thomas admitted. "I probably look a little green around the gills."

"You do," said Lars. "We've run through the snook here anyway. We should move on." He started the engine, letting Ben handle the steering wheel, and then left the console to move forward and pull up anchor. He took the wheel back from Ben and turned the boat south, parallel to the beach.

"It's rough out here on the Gulf side when it gets this windy," Lars shouted to them. "I have another place we can try to the south, through Captiva Pass, that's sheltered from the waves."

Within five minutes they had reached the southern tip of Cayo Costa. Lars turned the *Valhalla* east, bearing into the pass between Cayo Costa and North Captiva to the south. He throttled down and found the spot he was looking for, inside a small sand bar parallel to the island. After briefly studying the current, he cut the engine and moved forward to drop anchor. Ben took a moment to reach out and dip his hand into the water, marveling at its warmth.

"Let's give it a try here," Lars said. He began by chumming with some of the baitfish, tossing them into the water near the shore, where the current flowed the fastest. Lars gave a snort of disgust when there were no immediate takers. "We're not even attracting bait stealers," he said. "Looks like it's dead here." He raised the anchor and they moved several hundred yards farther to the northeast, closer to Pejuan Point, but after fifteen minutes with bait in the water and no hits, Lars decided they should leave.

"We should move on," he said with a touch of impatience in his voice. "It's likely we won't see much action for the next hour or so. We can head over to Cabbage Key and grab lunch."

"Sounds like a plan," Thomas responded.

"Are you feeling any better?" Ben asked Thomas.

"A lot better," he said. "I think getting out of that rough water worked." Thomas looked healthier; some color had come back into his face and he was no longer sweating so heavily.

"We can quit now," Ben said. "We can have lunch on Cabbage Key and then call it a day. There's no point staying out if you think you're going to be sick."

"No, I'm going to be okay. I've got some scopolamine in my bag that I can take; it should kick in fairly quickly."

"No need for heroics."

"There won't be any," he said, with a touch of annoyance.

They turned north, on a course that would take the *Valhalla* between Cayo Costa and the Intracoastal Waterway, back towards Cabbage Key and Useppa Island. Ben checked his watch: ten minutes after noon. Ben and Thomas stood on either side of the console, braced against the motion, both silenced by the engine's roar. Warm spray from the bow caught them in the face; Ben found it refreshing after the hours of relentless, mid-morning sun. Thomas reached across and tugged on Ben's sleeve, pointing to the starboard side of the *Valhalla* where two bottlenose dolphins had suddenly appeared. The dolphins followed the boat, their dorsal fins and flukes slicing through the water, before finally abandoning the chase. Ben gave Thomas a thumbs up, realizing the futility of trying to say anything over the engine noise, but wanting to share his appreciation of the moment.

The *Valhalla* had picked up speed and had begun to skim along the water on plane when Lars suddenly yelled for them to hold on; he swung the boat about to an abrupt stop.

"Damn, look at that," he said.

"At what?" Ben asked.

"Back there," he said, waving to indicate the southwest. "We spooked a school of tailing redfish back there. They're feeding on the island side between here and Pejuan Cove. Change of plans. We'll double back and I'll pole us in so we can take a crack at them."

"Are they heading for the mangroves along the shoreline?" Thomas asked, pointing to the fringe of mangroves on Cayo Costa.

"No, they won't congregate there this time of day. They're over in the Lake."

"The Lake?" Ben asked.

"It's just what the locals call it," Lars said. He jabbed his finger at the location on the waterproofed nautical chart Thomas always brought along to consult. "The Lake is a wide, shallow area inside of the sandbar there. The redfish are feeding there on clams and such when they're not hanging out in the potholes."

"We'll go without the engine from here on. I'll try to keep us from getting caught on the flats. When we get close enough to cast, I'll call out. Get the bait out in the middle of the school if you can, and let them swim by it."

The men stood at the stern of the boat, trying to spot the school ahead of them in the slick, glinting water. Lars had a better vantage point from the platform over the outboard engine. He scanned the surface from right to left before whistling in appreciation. "I see them," he said. "I see their tails. We're close enough to pole in next to them. It's a large school." Thomas handed him the long aluminum pole, careful not to let it bang or rattle against the sides of the boat.

Lars began poling, pushing the *Valhalla* forward with sweeping thrusts of the pole. His long-sleeved khaki shirt quickly became stained with sweat. He stopped poling once and paused to mop his face and beard with a small towel and to dry off the headband of his flat-billed Keys guide cap.

"Remember Mr. Charlevoix?" Thomas asked Ben. "Our Latin teacher in high school?"

"Sure," Ben said. He flashed Thomas a bemused look. "What in the world makes you bring him up now?"

"Lars, actually. Looking at him up there reminded me of an illustration from our Latin textbook, of Charon the bargeman, poling across the Styx, bringing Aeneas to the Underworld. '*Horrendus portior Charon, terribili squalore*'."

"You always had a great memory."

"I memorized that passage for class," he said. "The dreadful ferryman Charon, of frightful filth."

"Charon was dreadful but Mr. Charlevoix was a tough son of a bitch," Ben said. "I doubt there are too many teachers like him anymore in Bedford."

"It's strange what triggers my memory these days," Thomas said. "I'm watching Lars pole and all of a sudden the image of Charon and Aeneas form in my mind. I doubt I've given it a thought since high school. Until now. Thirty-five years go by and then the Latin phrase pops up in my head. A series of associations. I've had that same experience with patients, who remind me of people from the past. It seems that it's happening more often. The memories."

"I think I'm headed in the other direction," Ben told him. "Early Alzheimer's. There are whole parts of my past that I've forgotten. I think back and I draw a blank."

"That's a turn," Thomas said. "You're supposed to be the reflective one."

"I always get that label, don't I, Doctor Tom?"

"It fits, doesn't it?" Thomas said lightly. "Just as I'm supposed to be the scientist, the analytical one, oblivious to the emotional stuff. Believe me, I always hear it from Elaine when Darian calls and I want to know how her studies are going and I don't ask about her social life."

"So you concede that you're an insensitive prick?"

Thomas enjoyed the jibe. "For the most part," he said. "Except I'm getting sentimental as I get older. I must be losing brain cells."

"Is that a diagnosis?"

"No, that's a fact."

Lars' steady poling had moved them closer to Cayo Costa. His khaki shirt was now completely drenched from his exertion. The pole was sticking in the mucky bottom and Lars had to tug hard to pull it free for each push. But their slow progress had brought them closer to casting range of the school.

"They're right ahead of us," Lars called to them. " Don't move if you can help it, we want as little noise as possible. Cast right off the bow as far as you can when I tell you, and be quick about it."

He brought them closer with several vigorous pushes with the pole. Ben tensed in anticipation, gripping the cork rod-handle tightly. They were all excited. There was something primal about it, closing in on their prey.

"Cast now," Lars said. "They're at one o'clock." Ben cast his line with a high, arching action, hoping to get as much distance as possible, but when the bait hit the water it fell short of the school. "Reel it in and try again."

Thomas' cast was much better, perhaps twenty feet farther than Ben's. He had always been the better athlete, the tailback in high school to Ben's right tackle, the pitcher and shortstop to Ben's first baseman. But his cast also fell short. Lars kept poling, trying to maneuver them closer to the fish. Then there was a sudden thumping sound. The men turned back towards the noise and saw Lars grabbing at the pole: with his last push he had momentarily lost his balance and the pole had bumped the side of the *Valhalla*. The sound carried across the water; it was louder than Ben would have imagined. After righting himself and looking back at the surface, Lars cursed and told them that the fish had scattered.

"It figures," he said. "I'm hassling you two to keep quiet and I'm the one that screws up and spooks them."

"You're sure they're gone?" Thomas asked.

"Did you hear the thrashing out there after I lost the pole? They're long gone. Incredibly sensitive to any sound. I just hope they haven't been scared off to deep water. If they leave the Lake, we might as well pack it in and go get lunch."

Ben was secretly glad that it had been Lars' mistake, not his or Thomas'. Lars had little patience for clumsiness on the *Valhalla*. They had all heard the story of Lars' fishing trip with a visiting Hollywood actor who fancied himself an outdoorsman. Lars and the actor were drift fishing for tarpon in Boca Grande Pass on the Saturday before Memorial Day. Right away they had jumped a fish, and the movie star tried to hook the fish with a dramatic lunge of the rod. He lost him. Lars had muttered under his breath, but had held his notoriously short temper. Lars had instructed the actor, twice, to just let the fish take the bait and let Lars set the hook through the forward motion of the *Valhalla* when he gunned the engine.

He again explained to the actor what he should do and why. "If you try to set the hook too fast it'll pull right out of that tarpon's mouth," he said. "It's bony and lots of times the hook won't set, and then we've got nothing."

Fifteen minutes later another tarpon had attacked their drifting bait, this time jumping clear out of the water, its long silver body writhing in the air, before it plunged back into the murky waters of the pass. The actor whipped the rod up in the air, falling back in the captain's chair in his haste to hook the fish. In a moment the line went slack as the tarpon pulled free.

"Dammit," Lars said angrily. "Don't you listen?"

"I don't need you telling me how to fish."

"You're a fool," Lars told the man. "I don't have time for fools."

"I don't think you understand," the actor said. "I'm paying for this trip."

"No," Lars said. "Keep your money. The morning's on me, because we're heading back to the dock. Maybe you can find another guide stupid enough to waste his time with you. I won't."

"Maybe you don't realize who I am," the man said.

"I know who you are and I don't really care," Lars said, and then, delivering an insult that would be repeated for years among the guides. "I haven't been to a movie theater since John Wayne died, and you damn well haven't given me any friggin' reason to go back." (It was true, in a narrow sense, that Lars hadn't been to the movies, but his teenage daughter rented videos all the time and Lars occasionally watched. The actor didn't know that, however.)

Lars didn't talk to anyone about the confrontation, obeying the unwritten code of the professional fishing guide that you keep close-mouthed about your clients and their predilections, about the married men fishing with their "nieces," about the senile, and drunk and nasty. It was the movie star who provided the details to strangers, bitterly complaining about Lars to anyone on Boca Grande who would listen.

Ben suspected that Lars had secretly relished playing the role of redneck fishing guide. Lars had served in the Navy, travelling all over the world, earning two graduate degrees. He spent ten years in Annapolis, Maryland, and Norfolk, Virginia as a boat designer. He had returned to Florida when he was forty and became a fishing guide by choice.

Lars simply didn't like any mistakes on his boat, and he was even harsher on himself when he was to blame. He stopped cursing after a while, but his mouth remained set in a grim line.

"What's the plan now?" Thomas asked.

"Follow them, heading in the direction we saw those flurries," he said. "Can't risk the engine noise so I'll have to pole us there. My dad has tried using his electric trolling motor for reds but it doesn't work. It makes too much sound. Even that slight hum, the fish hear it and spook."

"How old is your dad?" Ben asked.

"Close to eighty. Still full of piss and vinegar."

"Still fishing?"

"Every day he can. He fishes off the dock because I won't let him go out in his boat alone, although I'm sure the old bastard sneaks out by himself once in a while."

Lars climbed back up onto the platform. He resumed poling the boat towards the school of redfish. In the far distance, to the east near Punta Gorda, they could see cumulus clouds forming in columns which, Ben knew, would slowly cluster into larger formations and produce thunderstorms later in the afternoon. The sky around them remained clear, however, and there were no immediate signs of bad weather.

Lars gave the pole a long, smooth push and as the *Valhalla* glided over the flats, told them in a lowered voice to watch out for signs of the redfish. After ten minutes of hard poling Ben spotted ten or fifteen reddish tails popping up in the water, betraying the school's location. They were feeding fifty feet or so to the starboard of the *Valhalla*.

"We're heading right into the midst of them," Lars told them, his good humor restored by the prospect. The day, and the trip, still had potential. He gingerly lowered himself to the deck of the skiff and carefully stowed away the pole.

"I'll cast first," he said, keeping his voice low. "This is as thick as I've seen them in a while. Years ago, before we had all this fishing pressure, you'd come across a school where the fish were so thick that the water would turn red. We don't have that, but this school is damn impressive."

Lars chose a rod from the under-gunwale rod storage and quickly, and efficiently, tied a weedless spoon to its leader. He braced himself and then cast the lure out to where he'd spotted the school. The cast had the effortless grace of a golf professional driving a tee-shot straight down the fairway. The spoon skipped several times across the water, its reflective sides flashing in the sun, before it sank from view. Lars handed the rod to Ben, and a redfish hit the lure almost immediately. The fish dove to the bottom and Ben knew that, unlike snook, the redfish on his line wouldn't surface again until the fish surrendered to exhaustion at the end of their battle. "Pull him this way, back to the boat," Lars instructed, "and the others should follow him."

Then, after baiting the hook with a sardine, Lars cast for Thomas. Lars had a guide's wariness of soft, indoor instincts. "Make sure you let the fish take the damn bait before you start cranking," he counseled Thomas. The results of his second cast were the same: a redfish took the bait almost at the moment Thomas accepted the rod in his hands, pulling the tip of the rod down towards the water and bending the fiberglass pole into a taut curve. Without pausing for long Lars cast with a third rod and, when he got a strike, began reeling in himself.

Ben was the first to bring his redfish to the boat. Lars exchanged rods with him, letting Ben continue to play Lars' hooked-up fish. Lars measured the first coppery-bronze fish and grimaced in disgust. "Too large," he said. "It's thirty-two inches, so we'll have to release her."

They had no luck with the other two redfish: Thomas' measured twenty-nine inches and Lars' was just shy of thirty. "Looks like the magic number is twenty-seven," Lars said. "We can keep them between eighteen and twenty-eight inches. We must have blundered into a bunch of bull redfish. Most of them will be too big. But we'll hook a legal one before long."

But Lars was wrong. After the *Valhalla* was anchored, they caught another ten redfish in a rally that lasted almost an hour, but none of the fish fit in the legal slot when they were measured. At one point it seemed to Ben that the entire school had decided to promenade past the boat, their long copper bodies marked with characteristic eye-like spots at the base of their squared-off tails. Lars gazed at them emotionlessly. Then, suddenly, they were gone. The men kept casting for ten minutes, hoping to attract a straggler or two, but the flats were quiet.

Lars stopped first. He didn't say anything for a long time, and then he climbed back onto the platform, gazing out over the lake, searching for the redfish. Ben looked at his watch: 4:35.

"Gentlemen, I'm afraid that's it," Lars said. "We've lost them. Now even if I did spot them, I don't think I could pole us close enough before we'd have to go. Sorry, but we're out of time."

"How far to Boca Grande from here?" Thomas asked.

"We're close enough so that we can beat the rain if we leave now," Lars replied.

Ben looked over his shoulder at the sky to the east. There was a line of thunderclouds and several bands of dark rain had begun sheeting down to the harbor.

"You can see that it's blowing this way," Lars said. "We should leave now. I'm sorry."

"No need to apologize," Thomas said. "We've had our chances."

"More than enough action for one day," Ben said.

Lars shook his head. "No keepers. That's a disappointment."

"No, it isn't," Thomas said quickly. Ben remained silent. "I've never seen redfish schooled up quite like that. It was marvelous. And we had a great rally there at the end, even if we didn't catch anything within the limit."

Lars shook his head again. "With all that poling, and chasing, and all that casting we should have hooked a couple of keepers. We brought enough to the boat. The law says you can take one each, and I hate for you to miss out on what's yours."

"We don't have to bring back a lot of fish," Thomas said. "That's not the point. We don't have to do that for this to be a great day fishing. A grand day, as my uncle Baldwin would say. And how many grand days are there? In a lifetime?"

Ben had a sudden flash of memory: of hunting for deer with Thomas in Bedford when they were teenagers. It was a crisp afternoon and the countryside offered the fading beauty of the late autumn in the Midwest. Their luck was bad—they never fired their rifles—but Thomas hadn't been disappointed. His reasoning had been the same then, that they might not have bagged a deer but they'd caught the fall show of red and gold leaves and blue sky. Then, as now, he had proclaimed it a grand day.

"You're the clients," Lars said. "If you're happy. . ." His voice trailed off, leaving the sentence unfinished. He shrugged and moved to the front of the *Valhalla* to retrieve the anchor.

"There are times I wish I could stay here out for the duration," Thomas said, turning to Ben. He spoke rapidly, the emotion apparent. "Fish every day, fish from first light until it's too dark to see. I'd catch every damn kind of fish in the harbor. Shoot for an in-shore Slam every day: redfish, snook, trout. Early summer I'd go for a Grand Slam: redfish, snook, trout and tarpon all in one day."

"It wouldn't take that long," Lars said. He finished pulling the anchor out of the bay, its flukes stained with bottom muck, and looked over at Thomas. Lars seemed surprised, almost embarrassed, by Thomas' sudden display of fervor; it had been unexpected coming from him. Lars prided himself on knowing his clients. "I could get you there in a week, or less if we had any luck. If you're willing to drift fish for tarpon at night in the Pass, getting that Grand

Slam becomes a lot easier. I don't like doing it because of all the amateurs out there running around at night, without a clue. You spend half of your time dodging the fools. But it certainly improves your odds."

"I'd be in no rush," Thomas said. It was clear to Ben that he had a mental picture of what he wanted to do, and wasn't interested in altering it. "I'm convinced that at the end I'd have mastered it. I'd know the patterns of the fish, where they hide, where they are at given times of day. I'd think like a fish, not that they think in the way we do, because they don't have much in the way of higher intelligence."

"About as much as the tourists," said Lars with a wolfish grin.

"Ah, the tourists," Thomas said. "There's a strange symbiosis for you. Our Florida economy here depends on them, but all of us can't wait for them to clear out when the season is over."

"No different than the college students in Bloomington," Ben said. "Except the kids remind you of how old you've become."

Lars moved over to the console, scanning the flats around them one last time before he started the engine. They were silent the rest of the way as Lars drove them across south of the Pass, skimming the crests. Within fifteen minutes they were in sight of the Boca Grande lighthouse. Another ten minutes brought them to the inlet near Miller's and Lars slowed to steer the *Valhalla* through the channel. Lars offered a casual wave to the golfers on the Gasparilla Inn course as they wended their way to the marina.

After he had tied the boat off at the dock, Lars took the ice chest off the boat and carried it over to the sinks by the dock to gut and clean the fish. Two pelicans flapped over to the water by the dock; they were regulars, waiting to scavenge the fish bodies and unfilleted remains of the catch. Thomas fooled with the flight bag he'd brought along, lingering aboard the *Valhalla*.

"It's too bad the day has to end," he said. "Next time let's stay out later, even if we have to pay Lars a little more. It's the summer so there shouldn't be any rush."

"We could do that," Ben said. "You want to grab a beer in Miller's before we head back to clean up and collect the girls?"

"Sounds good," he said. Thomas turned and gazed curiously across the water and towards the horizon, almost as if he was looking for something. "Ben, before we go in, I have a favor to ask."

"Sure," Ben said. "Ask away."

"This would be easy for you," he said. "I mean if the roles were reversed, because I'm not the reflective type. I'm not used to dwelling on things, on worrying."

Ben laughed. "That's why my mother thought you should be the one to become an astronaut. Not me. This was freshman year of college when I had decided that I should be the next John Glenn. I came back at Christmas break and Mom loved the idea—for you. Remember? She said I'd worry too much.

Was the rocket going to explode on the launch pad at Cape Canaveral? Was the heat shield going to burn up? Thomas wouldn't worry, she said, he'd be too busy calculating the angle of ascent or thinking of new on-board experiments."

"She had me right. That's why I've always loved surgery. You don't overthink. You review the X-rays, assess, make your notes and then do the surgery. There's no room for Hamlet in the O.R."

Ben knew better than to interrupt his friend again. Thomas would get to the point in his own way, without prompting. His friend took his hat off and ran his hand through his hair before he continued.

"I tried to talk to Elaine about this last week, before we came over to Boca Grande, but she wasn't very receptive. She won't have the conversation, and you know when she doesn't want to talk there's no way you can force it. That's why I'm talking to you now."

Ben didn't say anything. He had made it a practice to steer clear of disputes between his friends and their wives. He found they had a better chance of staying friends that way. Early in his legal career he had decided to avoid the acrimonious entanglements of matrimonial law, and now he hoped Thomas wouldn't entangle him in anything awkward. During all the years they had known the Staffords he'd seen no more than the normal tensions a married couple experiences.

"How can I help?"

"Sorry," Thomas said, "I know that this whole discussion is out of the clear blue."

"Don't worry about that."

"You see, I'm going to sell my practice and shift over to teaching." He cleared his throat. "I've been putting my financial house in order the last couple of months with Johnson Nees, my attorney in Winter Haven. We updated my will last month, and I had Johnson put in it that I'm to be cremated. And I want my ashes spread out there." He motioned in the broad direction of the harbor. "I've specified that in my will, that it'd be in the harbor. After today, I think I even know the location where I'd like to be scattered. Where we found the school of redfish."

"The Lake?"

"The Lake," he said. "But I need someone to actually take a boat out there and follow through. The scattering part. I don't really feel comfortable asking anyone else."

"You want me in the boat."

"That's it."

"Is Elaine going to be all right with this?"

"Not with the cremation part. But you're the only choice for the scattering. I'll just tell her and Johnson that you are going to handle it."

Ben looked out back towards the harbor, shielding his eyes from the late afternoon sun. The clouds had scudded closer and now loomed in a dark sullen mass to the east. They were closing in on the western end of the harbor, and the air felt moist and heavy. The breeze had turned cooler, promising a storm ahead. He turned back to Thomas. Five years earlier Ben would have joked with him, laughed at his idea, but he knew he couldn't deflect the request now. Perhaps reaching your late fifties forced you to consider the unthinkable, Ben thought. He knew that he would agree, that he had to agree, to Thomas' request.

Thomas spoke again, before Ben could respond. "Elaine won't do it herself," he said. "She hates the idea of cremation. Too much the Catholic, I guess."

"I thought the church had relaxed that rule."

"The church may have, but Elaine hasn't. She can't handle the idea of my death, which is funny in a strange way. She's the one who buys into eternal life. I'm the skeptic about exactly what awaits us. The death part, the mechanical part, doesn't faze me in the least. An occupational benefit. You see enough of anything and you lose the fear, or at least most of it. I'm in no hurry for the experience, mind you, but I feel like it's time to put things in place. So I need your help. That's my favor, then."

Ben looked over at Lars. Their guide had finished cleaning the fish and was smoking a cigarette by the table, under the shade of the overhanging balcony of Miller's, not wanting to intrude into whatever was being discussed on his boat. Lars would wait for his clients to finish. Ben thought about the dark coolness of the second floor of Miller's, and the taste of his first beer.

"In the Lake?" he asked. "I think I can find the spot with a little help from Lars. If it ever comes to that, and you beat me to the finish line."

"Thanks. That makes this the perfect day."

"Even without catching a redfish?"

"Especially without catching one," Thomas said. "Now I'm sort of glad that we left them there back in the Lake. It would have disturbed things if we'd kept any. It would have unbalanced things somehow."

"I don't completely follow you," Ben said. "But I wouldn't repeat that to Lars. He'll think that you're coming unhinged."

"I don't expect you to completely understand," Thomas said. "I'm not sure I do, myself."

Together they walked back to the dock to pay Lars and thank him for the day. He seemed ill-at-ease. Ben wondered whether Lars had overhead any of their conversation, or if he was just anxious about avoiding the thunderstorm. While Lars finished policing his boat, Thomas stored the filleted mangrove snapper in the small cooler (watched with greedy eyes by the scavenger pelicans). Lars wasted no time in casting off, and they watched him back the *Valhalla* away from the dock, and then with a wave, motor swiftly from the marina towards the bayou and the open water of the harbor. He would have to hurry to beat the edge of the storm.

After they had lost sight of the skiff, Thomas tapped Ben lightly on the shoulder, an affectionate tap. "You know, I don't worry about the end game anymore," he said. "I figure that in the end, we're meant to accept it. The inevitable. The best for last, Uncle Baldwin would say, the best is always saved for last. We shouldn't rage against the dying of the light, or whatever the phrase is."

"The dying of the light."

"I don't mean to be morbid," he said. "But I figured that you'd be willing to listen."

Thomas gazed back towards Boca Grande Pass and Cayo Costa to the southwest. His face had softened; his sharp, usually intense features had a relaxed, almost vulnerable, look and Ben found himself thinking how little Thomas' looks had changed over time. It was past time to go, but they stood there together, joined in their memories and in their reluctance to bring their grand day on the water to a close.

"Those redfish were magnificent, weren't they?" Thomas said, savoring the sound of the adjective, repeating it slowly. "Magnificent."

"That they were, Doctor Tom," Ben said. "That they were."

11

The Book Finder

Perhaps my favorite childhood bedtime storybook was *The Golden Cockerel*, a retelling of Alexander Pushkin's poetic fairy tale.

It wasn't just the story—which featured a fat and jovial king who loved his feather bed, an evil sorcerer, two beautiful princesses, and a magic rooster—but the exotic illustrations in the book that fascinated me. They featured romantic and elegant scenes, drawn in the Art Nouveau style with sinuous curves and deep, vivid colors—burgundy, green, gold, purple. I could study these pictures for hours.

I would pester my father to read the book again and again to me. I'm sure that he must have been bored to tears by the repetition, but he hid it well, adding to the book's natural suspense with his dramatic reading.

Those are the clearest memories I have of him, now, his half-glasses perched on his nose, his deep bass voice resonating as he read, his smile when we came to the part of the story where the courtiers and the royal blacksmith struggled to fit the portly King Dadon in his old suit of armor.

We only had a few years together.

When I had my own children, and began reading to them at bedtime, I thought about *The Golden Cockerel*. While my daughters enjoyed the books then in fashion—*Goodnight, Moon* and *Where the Wild Things Are*—I wanted to share my favorite with them.

But I couldn't find a copy. I had no luck in the local public library, nor in any of the local bookstores I tried. When I traveled to New York or Chicago or San Francisco on business I would haunt the children's sections of the booksellers there, on the lookout for *The Golden Cockerel*. I found a few versions of the tale, but not the one I wanted.

Finally I gave up. And by then my girls were beyond picture books.

Like many my age, I am ambivalent about the Internet. It has not been an unalloyed boon to mankind as its breathless, technology-worshipping acolytes would have us believe. Unless you're willing to argue for the merits of better enabling compulsive shoppers, seekers of hard-core porn, and members of the Aryan Brotherhood trolling for followers.

But I learned that the Web also made it possible to find out-of-print books, through websites like Alibris and Bookfinder. So I began searching for my lost book, looking for copies printed before 1950, the year of my birth.

The first children's version of Pushkin's tale that matched my criteria was published by The Heritage Press in, of all years, 1950. I ordered it from an online bookseller and it arrived within days. I opened the bubble-wrapped package eagerly and rapidly flipped through the pages of the book, hunting for the illustrations.

There was a marvelous image of King Dadon lounging in his feather bed, but I was disappointed. It wasn't the book from my childhood. The Heritage Press illustrator, Edmund Dulac, drew and painted in the Art Nouveau style, but his sense of composition was tighter, more ordered than what I had remembered. Moreover, there were only a few pictures scattered throughout the book where my lost book had been crammed full of art.

I tried again. This time I found a version with a 1938 copyright, written by Elaine Pogany with pictures by Willy Pogany. It took longer for the book to arrive, and when it did, it carried a "DISCARD" stamp from the public library of Virginia, Minnesota. (I looked it up and Virginia is located in the northeastern part of the state, on the Mesabi Range. They hold a Land of the Loon Festival there every year.)

I knew it was *the* book the moment I saw the black-and-white illustration of helmeted warriors on the opening pages. I leafed through it, delighted to find the images matched what was in my mind's eye: fat white-bearded King Dadon, the wicked Magician of the Dark Mountains, the pretty young Princess Tatiana, and the mysterious Princess Shamaka. There was the dark cave where the Magician studied old books by the light of a million fireflies, and the field of soldiers, including the King's beloved son Prince Igor, turned to stone by the sorcerer's spell. And there was the proud Golden Cockerel, with his sweeping tail feathers and crimson comb.

It was like finding a long-lost friend and discovering that you could pick up from your last conversation as if it had only been days since you had last talked, not decades.

You might well ask why finding *The Golden Cockerel* mattered so much to me. Perhaps you haven't felt the pull of nostalgia, the desire to revisit the past, to explore old memories. If you have, then you can know how compelling the call can be.

I am self-aware enough to know that I cannot fully trust my memories of those few years my father was with us. No doubt I have idealized that time, seeing it as a golden period in my life, imbuing it with greater significance that it perhaps deserved. And losing my father when I did, when I was ten years old, means that I imagine him solely from the perspective of a young boy. He remains a larger-than-life figure in my imagination, never subjected to a teenager's hyper-critical judgment.

I keep my copy of *The Golden Cockerel* in my top right desk drawer in my study at home. I glance at it perhaps once a year, typically as Christmas and the New Year approaches. That is when I find myself thinking about the course of my life and those moments when I felt most loved and could love freely in return.

It may seem a strange keepsake to some, this slightly worn-out children's book—although perhaps not any stranger than Charles Foster Kane's Rosebud—but I have long since stopped worrying about the opinions of others.

My daughters know about the book, and why it has such meaning and value for me. I am confident that when I die one of them will want it as a memento of her father. Will it be passed down to her children as a reminder? Perhaps, but I suspect that by then its power—now third-hand— will have faded, along with the colors in those marvelous ornately elegant illustrations.

12

Last Pond

The nearby neighborhoods hadn't changed appreciably, except that they seemed smaller. *Didn't everything seem smaller*, he thought, savoring his own middle-aged cynicism. It sounded like the punch line to one of the raunchy jokes Angus collected when he went pub-crawling.

The rental car, a cheap Ford Taurus, struggled to maintain speed as he drove it up Miller Hill Road, past the skyline of lean pine trees and occasional boulders to where he knew the pond was located. There had never been many houses there, and he was pleased to see that new houses hadn't been jammed in by inventive developers. It'd been more than fifteen years since he'd been back, and despite the reports from a distant uncle of a local real estate boom, it clearly hadn't extended to the outskirts of the town.

Curtis had first planned this visit to his childhood hometown six months earlier. He was there, oddly enough, because of a chance conversation in a shabby African hotel on a Monday filled with bad news. The local political situation had deteriorated over the weekend before. Hopes of a truce between the ruling clique of thugs and rebel forces had collapsed. There were reports of ambushes and lawlessness on the outskirts of the capital, a coveted prize for both sides.

There was more specific bad news, as well. The arrival of promised medical supplies for the Center had been delayed. Curtis had been told that there was engine trouble with the chartered plane, but the real trouble was that the pilot didn't want to risk the sporadic small arms fire that had been greeting inbound flights for the last week. Curtis didn't blame him.

And Montgomery had stopped by to confirm the worst news of all, about Joseph, one of their drivers, a favorite of both Curtis and Angus. Joseph's body had been found four miles outside the capital city; he had been shot in the back of the head and robbed, his pockets turned out, his wallet and Center ID card missing. Curtis was dismayed: he'd held out the slim hope that Joseph's disappearance had a benign explanation.

Curtis had retreated to what passed for a lounge in the hotel and took three bottles of beer over to a table and began drinking. He had finished his second bottle when a young physician, Mereille Desrosiers, of Medecin San Frontiers, came over to his table.

"Curtis," she said. He acknowledged her with a wave of his beer bottle. "Drinking alone? Where's Angus?"

"He flew down to Jay-burg. Gone for a week. So I'm abandoned."

"That's bad. You know that you should always have company when you drink. Let me join you."

He gestured to the empty chair across from him. She was pretty in a gamine way, her hair cut boyishly short, her clothes stylish. While Curtis found himself attracted to her, he also knew that Mereille already had a lover, one of the female doctors. Gossip about both romantic attachments and sexual entanglements (which were separate phenomena) spread quickly in the NGO enclave.

"Please do," Curtis said. "I've got a plan tonight. Very simple plan. Based on drinking enough beer in a short enough period of time. I want to wake up tomorrow with a hangover so bad I can't remember today."

He put out his cigarette (Mereille was sensitive to smoke) and got to his feet awkwardly and went over to the bar to get her a bottle, and a clean glass. She drank beer, he remembered, which made it easier. The bar always seemed to have chilled beer, which was one of the few things they got right. The hotel had been run by Hilton once, and then had been nationalized. It was said that the president's nephew held a controlling interest. Curtis bought three more bottles and asked the bartender for two glasses.

"Rough one?" she asked when he had returned.

"We lost Joseph."

"I'm sorry," she said.

He poured beer into their glasses and handed her one.

"I'd been expecting the worst for the last few days. The car turned up before Joseph did. They abandoned it by the airport when they ran out of gas."

"I think I met him once," she said.

"A good man. A good driver."

"It was the rebels?"

"Who knows? It could have been them. It could have been our so-called friends with the so-called government. It could have been someone freelancing. I don't think it particularly matters to Joseph."

"I'm sorry," she said.

"Aren't we all?" Curtis asked. He waved in the direction of the door. "We have the ultimate advantage, don't we? When it gets bad enough there's always the airport. We show our passport, hop aboard the next plane, and fly out of here without a second thought."

"It's not that easy," she said. "Otherwise you wouldn't still be here."

Curtis kept silent.

"It bothers all of us," she said. "The massive stupidity of it. The waste. The pain. It doesn't make much sense. I concede that."

"So how do you make sense of it?"

"I'll tell you how I've kept my sanity," Mereille said. "If I'm sane, and I'm sure that my colleagues trained in psychiatry might question that. It's a very common technique. They teach it in all the meditation classes. To relieve stress I visualize. *J'imagine le plaisir.* Not world peace. That's complete *merde.* I wouldn't waste my time on that. The more time I spend here, the more I think John and Yoko were full of crap. You better come damn well armed if you want to give peace a chance. No, I think of something more practical, a boulangerie on Rue Charlotte near my aunt's apartment, and I imagine the croissants and bread they make there. I can smell the bread baking and I think about the taste of those croissants, how flaky the crust is, and it helps."

"You find that helps?"

"Crazy. I know. But it helps. Whenever I get back home I go to that boulangerie. I buy half-a-dozen croissants, a few with *chocolat*, and I take them back to my mother's place and I eat them all. In one sitting." She laughed. "It makes me sick. But it's home and it's rational, a civilized place and it's something to look forward to no matter how horrible it gets here. *C'est une ancre.* An anchor."

Mereille, despite her small size, kept up with him beer for beer. They got drunk together, and he found the oblivion he wanted that night and the distraction of an awful hangover the next morning.

For several days afterward he gave some thought to Mereille's coping mechanism. He had seen many of the diplomats, relief workers, journalists and UN types lose themselves in sex, drugs, and rock n' roll: the Expats' Trinity for the dead time, for the off-hours. Others couldn't deal with the grinding reality and the daily fear and despair and they found a way to cut their time short and leave, to escape.

A few adopted a neo-colonialist position of detached superiority. "What do you expect?" asked one Austrian, a tall, bitter man named Rolf. "They're not ready to govern. You don't have to be here long to figure that out. And that's not racialist. It's fact. I was in Liberia when the marvelous Sergeant Doe assumed power in 1985. He marched the old government leaders out onto the beach and tied them to posts and had them shot. Very direct way of showing his displeasure, wouldn't you say?"

Curtis would always mumble about Bosnia and Northern Ireland and that Africans didn't have a monopoly on tribalism, but he didn't really want to debate the matter. What would it prove? He found himself wishing that he had Angus' sharp wit, for Angus always quickly deflated the cocktail-hour pontificators with a stinging comment or two.

"I'll tell you the problem," Rolf continued. "We're all here as a half-measure. All the NGOs. The UN. All the fucking alphabet people. We band-aid the disease. We don't have the balls to do it right, to bring in the troops and govern this place as a protectorate. That wouldn't look good. We'd be taking up the White Man's burden. But if we can't do that, we ought to get out."

"I don't know," Curtis said, shaking his head.

"I do know," said Rolf. "We need to abandon our illusions. They're dangerous, I tell you, they're dangerous."

Curtis saw no point in arguing about the "situation on the ground"—to use Angus' term—with Rolf, or with anyone else. He had given up on making much sense of the current situation. He worried that he was giving up on more than that. There had been a time when he was fiercely proud of what he and his colleagues at the Center did—he knew that he'd brought some order, some hope to the places they'd been sent. But he had begun to wonder whether Rolf had gotten some of it right, that they had become ineffectual, that they were offering Band-Aids to a part of the world that was hemorrhaging from fear and madness.

He welcomed not thinking about it. It was best to adopt Mereille's form of psychic escape, and he decided after a week of visualizing that it worked.

Curtis would lie on his bed and try to block out the sound of his rickety air conditioner and drift back to the same place, Last Pond, and the same time, the winter afternoons when he and Ned and Frenchie and the O'Connor brothers would play pick-up hockey games, pond hockey.

In his mind he would trace their route from his house, past the railroad tracks, under the bridge, up Miller Hill to the line of trees and the pond, hidden from view at the top. They would abandon their boots and shoes and eagerly lace up their skates and choose up teams, pretending to be their heroes: Bobby Orr and Tony Esposito of the Bruins, Rocket Richard of the Canadiens, Bobby Hull and Phil Esposito and Stan Mikita of the Black Hawks.

Curtis loved being Bobby Orr, poke checking the puck away from an attacker and dashing up ice in a headlong rush, deking out the other skaters and finally flipping a quick wrist shot past the goalie and scoring. One Christmas his parents gave him a black-and-gold Bruins sweater with number 4 on it and he wore it proudly to the pond games, giving him, he argued, first claim on being Bobby Orr.

He was amazed at the details he could recall, and remembered reading once that whatever the mind kept and retained for long-term memories would be especially vivid.

He had a vacation coming, and he knew he needed to take some time, to get away, to gain a bit of perspective. Angus encouraged him to take a month off; he reminded Curtis that he wouldn't be helping anyone, or the Center, if he burned out.

So he bought round-trip tickets back to the United States, flying through Johannesburg and then to Atlanta, and forced himself to leave at the appointed time. His flight was inevitably delayed and when he arrived at customs in

Miami he found himself tired and cranky. He still had the flight to Atlanta to reach his family, which didn't improve his mood any, nor had sitting on airplanes that prohibited smoking.

He spent a miserable week with his sister, Janice, and his brother-in-law and their two kids. They lived ten miles or so from his parents in a suburban development, a cul de sac. Janice seemed tired all the time, and they had little to say to each other. Curtis, bored during the days, went on long walks. The houses and streets all looked the same to him, all fake colonials with large driveways and front lawns.

He knew that the comparisons between the suburban comfort of his sister and her neighbors and the misery he'd left behind were trite. Janice wasn't responsible for the nightmare conditions in Africa, nor could he blame her for her ignorance about what was going on. That few in the First World knew, or cared, about the tragedies of the Third World was a fact, nothing more. If Angus had been there he would have reminded Curtis that it had always been that way, and that not until the end of the twentieth century had television and CNN given the haves any sense of what the have nots struggled with. But Angus wasn't there.

Curtis couldn't talk to his parents, either. He spent most of his vacation time with them, in their ranch house in Marietta. He was glad there was a television in the guest bedroom where he was left undisturbed. He watched for hours, chain-smoking, amazed at the sheer mindlessness of the soaps and Jerry Springer and the all-sports channels, a new feature since his last visit, and he was somehow delighted by it all.

His mother was well meaning enough, but he knew she wouldn't understand how he felt. He didn't want to confuse and upset her with his own conflicted feelings. With his father, it was a different matter. He would understand, but Curtis wouldn't burden him with his own sadness and doubts.

His father approached him after Curtis had been there a week. "I guess it's been pretty bad over there," his father said matter-of-factly as if he was discussing the state of the Braves' bullpen.

"Yes."

"I've seen some of it on the television news," he said. "I can't watch it for too long. If your mother is around she gets too worked up. She starts to cry. Especially when the kids are shown."

"It's pretty rugged."

"She worries about you, Curtis."

"I can take care of myself," Curtis said. "I've been doing this for a while."

"That's what I tell her. But she worries."

"I appreciate that, Pop. But I'm copacetic."

His father looked at him, weighing something, and then he responded. "I guess you know I saw some hard things myself. In Vietnam."

Curtis nodded. His father had been a seventeen-year-old kid from Lowell, Massachusetts who had never been south of Boston before the war took him to Asia.

"At first I felt guilty about surviving. It didn't seem right. That can be hard to live with."

"I know," Curtis said.

"But you go on. You don't forget but you find a way to go on. You're living. I guess you can't quarrel with that. You're alive."

Curtis nodded. He thought back to a roadblock where Joseph had talked their way past the teenage irregulars brandishing Karishnikovs. The guards were just nervous kids—in Marietta they would still be too young to drink. But in West Africa and Central Africa they had semiautomatic weapons and the occasional stripped, lifeless bodies left by the side of the road testified that they knew how to use them. Joseph's luck ran out; Curtis' had not.

"That's all I wanted to say," his father said. "For what it's worth."

"Thanks," Curtis said.

Curtis had planned his visit to Boston for his third week back in the US. He wanted to make sure that Last Pond was frozen over, and he figured that late January would be the best time.

He settled on a day trip. He just wanted to see the pond, to skate for a little while, and then turn around and head back to Atlanta. So he bought a ticket on the earliest Delta nonstop to Boston. He planned to rent a car at Logan, drive over to his old hometown, skate for a few hours and then maneuver through the evening rush hour traffic to get back in time to make an early-evening return flight. With any luck he'd be back at his parents' house by midnight.

He'd found his old Bauer hockey skates in one of his suitcases in his parents' garage. He transferred them to an L.L. Bean carry-on bag along with a pair of thick socks.

The flight north proved uneventful. He slept most of the way and woke when they landed at Logan. He found the restroom and changed into long underwear, blue jeans, two layers of T-shirts and a heavy-duty fleece. He had the car rental agent show him on the map the fastest return route to the Avis lot because he figured that he would be pressed for time when he drove back for his flight.

Within an hour he was driving through strangely familiar neighborhoods. He had forgotten how dingy and forlorn the town looked in winter. Along Main Street's small commercial strip the stores had changed. A video store had replaced the small grocery market and a delicatessen had displaced the town's pharmacy. He stopped in the deli and bought a cup of coffee, a tuna fish sandwich, and a carton of Marlboros.

He didn't stay long on Main Street; he was eager to reach Last Pond, so called because it was in the northwest corner of the town, on the highest point. First Pond was in the southeastern portion of the town, near the Common and the eighteenth-century Congregational church that the town was best known for. Curtis thought there was a sly Yankee humor in having first and last ponds. If you didn't live in the town you might not know about Last Pond. A fair number of the commercially available road maps overlooked it, because it was so small.

He followed Main Street for five blocks and then turned north by the VFW hall. A Civil War cannon and a World War I howitzer still sat on the front lawn there. Curtis drove under the railroad bridge, noting that teenagers were still spray-painting their initials on the black steel structure, before driving up Miller Hill Road, the only way to reach Last Pond by car.

Curtis was surprised to find the pond was still ringed by a dirt road—he had expected it would have been paved in the years since he had left. He remembered there were three houses, and was pleased to see his memory hadn't failed him.

Before refrigeration there had been an icehouse at Last Pond where the ice had been carved into blocks and stored. The icehouse had burned down sometime in the late 1940s but its brick foundation remained standing to the southeast of the pond.

Curtis parked the car by the side of the road. He sat in the passenger seat for a moment, enjoying the silence. He sipped his coffee and unwrapped the sandwich and ate it slowly. When he finished, he brushed the crumbs off his fleece and put the empty coffee cup and sandwich wrapper in the paper bag and put the bag on the passenger seat. Finally he put on a knit black cap, pulling it over his ears. He didn't want to return to Atlanta with frostbite. He smoked a cigarette, slowly, enjoying the feel of the smoke in his mouth and throat.

Curtis opened the door and stretched his legs out into the road. He pulled his shoes and socks off, wincing at the cold, and quickly put on the heavy woolen socks. He slid the skates onto his feet, tugging at the leather, and then carefully tightened the laces.

He negotiated his way from the car to the edge of the pond and gingerly stepped onto the ice, keeping his balance. There were no marks on the ice. He was the first to disturb the surface of the pond that day. He pushed off and began skating, feeling awkward and vulnerable, hoping to get the feel of the ice in his first tentative strides. He could feel the first trickles of sweat under his armpits. He skated in wider and wider circles, swooping close to the shoreline. He pretended he was playing shinny, dashing up the ice with the puck on his stick, chased by all the other skaters, and was surprised at how fast he could skate after so many years away.

Curtis savored the cold air and the slight discomfort when he took a deep breath. He wasn't used to the cold and the smoking meant his wind wasn't very good. He could see the moisture coming out of his mouth in a cloud. The ice had frozen solid and it didn't creak or groan under his weight. Curtis had been monitoring the Boston temperatures for the past week, hoping it would stay in the twenties at night. He knew the pond froze quickly and its surface stayed frozen longer than the other ponds in town.

Last Pond had been formed by the massive forces of an Ice Age glacier, which had carved out a bowl-shaped depression in the rock that made up Miller Hill. Because of that, and an overhanging tree canopy, Last Pond maintained a low temperature year round. There was more sunlight at noon, when the sun was directly overhead, but most of the time the pond was shaded. It was the first body of water in town to freeze, and the last to thaw out in the spring.

Last Pond had always seemed, in some mysterious way, to be linked more closely to the forces of nature than other places. As a boy it seemed to Curtis that the wind blew harder, the ice froze quicker, and snow fell faster at Last Pond. He remembered once, near the end of a day playing hockey, when without warning it began to snow quite heavily. Soon the snow was falling so hard and so fast that the boys had difficulty seeing each other or the puck. They had to abandon their game and hurry back down the hill and head for home, where a warm dinner waited for them.

"Something else," Frenchie said in awe as they left. "This is something else."

Curtis had never seen a heavier snowfall in a shorter time period, a freakish event if he ever experienced one, now linked permanently in his memory with the pond. He wondered what had happened to Frenchie and the others. They were probably townies still, plumbers and mechanics and electricians. Or maybe employees of the Department of Public Works.

He was brought back to the present by someone yelling. Curtis spun around on his skates to try to find the source of the noise.

"Hey," a man yelled at him. "Hey." He was excited, waving his arms and beckoning to Curtis. It was clear that ignoring him wouldn't work, so Curtis slowly skated over to the edge of the pond, reluctant to leave the center and the smooth ice. He could feel the cold pinching his cheeks and nose.

"Over here," the man said belligerently. He wore a faded, scarlet and black plaid hunting jacket. He needed a shave. White and gray stubble covered his chin, giving him a grizzled, unkempt look. He had red-rimmed dark eyes. "Didn't you see the sign?"

"The sign," Curtis repeated. "What sign?"

"Over there." The man pointed at a tree to the left of the spot where Curtis had parked the Taurus. Curtis focused on the spot and he could see red type on a white background. "This is private property. The pond is. We can't have people skating here without permission."

"I'm sorry," Curtis said. "I didn't see the sign. I used to skate here when I was a kid. We played pond hockey. I haven't been back in years."

"I've been here ten years," the man said, skeptically. "We've had the sign there all that time."

"Well, it's been longer than that," Curtis said, annoyed, remembering the instinctive, reflexive hostility of the locals towards outsiders. He had been a local once himself. "Twenty years. More than twenty years."

"These days just the people who live around the pond skate here. And that's not very often. If you want to skate, you go to the rink. I own the house over there." The man jerked his thumb towards the north and the smallest of the houses. "We've had it posted and kept the swimmers and skaters off all that time. There hasn't been any hockey in a long time, that's for sure. It's the liability."

"The liability?"

"All we need is for some kid to break a leg or fall through the ice and drown. They'd sue all of us. It's the damn lawyers." He cleared his throat. "Bastards."

"I wasn't planning to sue." Curtis said. He felt he needed to give the man a better explanation. "I haven't been back here in the winter in more than twenty years. I grew up down the way. Our house was on School Street. I was in Boston and thought I'd sneak out here and skate. For old-times' sake."

"You don't look like the type," the man said.

"The type to skate for old-times' sake?"

"No, the type to sue."

"You're right about that. I haven't ever sued anybody."

The man studied him for a moment. "Where did you say you were from?"

"Atlanta, now," Curtis said. "Just in Boston for the day. Like I said, I just had the impulse to come skate on the pond."

"You say you haven't been back for years," the man said. Curtis could see him reconsidering the situation.

"We moved away after high school. My parents ended up in Atlanta. I went to school in New York. Been working overseas but I live in Atlanta when I'm back in the States. Just haven't had the time to come up here."

The man looked at him curiously. "When was the last time you skated?"

"Maybe five years ago. In Atlanta." Curtis felt the need to say more. "They have rinks in Atlanta now."

"The kids don't skate outdoors much anymore," the man said. "They all go to the indoor rink down off 128. It's open round the clock."

"I guess they don't pretend to be Bobby Orr anymore, either," Curtis said. "Like I did."

"Bobby Orr. He was a helluva player. Everyone was crazy about hockey back then."

"We were," Curtis said. "All of us." He pointed to the pond. "We must have won the Stanley Cup a hundred times out there."

Curtis could see that the man's anger had passed. "Go ahead and finish your skate," the man said. "Don't worry about the other neighbors. You won't be bothered. They let me play bad cop."

"Thanks," Curtis said. The man waved at him and walked away towards the tree line, back towards his house.

Curtis skated back to the middle of the pond. He felt stiff from standing and talking to Last Pond's self-appointed guardian, and he could feel some pain in his ankles. He resolved to ignore it; he could always take some Tylenol for the flight home.

He began skating in large, swooping circles, enjoying the sound of the blades scraping against the ice and the sight of the lines that his skates were carving in the ice.

It was enough, he decided. It wasn't an epiphany or a complete counterbalance to all the pain of the last eighteen months, but it was enough. Mereille would laugh at him when he saw her again and he told her about his afternoon of skating on a small pond in a tired New England town as his therapy for burn-out. But it had been enough.

Curtis looked back to the shoreline and saw that the older man had returned. He was standing by the pond's edge close to Curtis' car, waiting to catch his eye. When Curtis skated over, he could see the man was holding a long steel thermos in both hands.

"I brought some hot coffee," the man said. "Thought you might like a cup."

"That's kind of you," said Curtis, surprised and pleased at the gesture. "That's great."

"Nothing beats a hot cup of coffee on a day like today."

The man unscrewed the cap and poured some coffee into a plastic cup. Curtis took the cup from him. "It's got a little half-and-half," he said. "Cuts down on the bitterness."

"That's fine." Curtis brought the cup to his lips and delighted in the fragrant smell. The first sip burned his tongue, but the hot liquid warmed his throat and chest. He risked a larger swallow. He cupped both hands around the cup and felt the warmth on his fingers. He fought the urge to light up a cigarette.

"Solomon Page," the man said, nodding at Curtis, who belatedly realized that the man was introducing himself.

"Curtis Muir."

The man bobbed his head in response.

"They used to cut up pond ice and sell it," he said. "They used saws to cut the blocks and then they'd drag or slide these huge blocks of ice over to the icehouse with heavy metal tongs. They'd take the ice and wrap it in sawdust and ship it all over the world. Sent it on clipper ships. Probably not from here, from this pond. It's too small. I think they just used the ice here, from Last Pond, in town."

"They stored it in the icehouse, didn't they?"

"That's what I've been told. I'd imagine that without the icehouse nobody would have come up here. Too far from the center of town. They didn't build these houses until the nineteen twenties, when they had autos."

"I envy you," Curtis said. "It is so incredibly peaceful up here."

"I only bought the house because of the pond. Paid more than I should have, but I liked the idea of looking out the living room window and being able to see water. It's peaceful, like you said. Calming."

Curtis could see that Page was enjoying the conversation. He guessed that the man was retired and wondered how much contact he had with anyone other than his neighbors. He checked his watch and saw that he was running out of time if he was to make his flight back to Atlanta.

"Time to go," Curtis said. He handed the plastic cup back to the older man and opened the car door so he could sit down and begin unlacing his skates. "Thanks for the coffee, and thanks for letting me skate."

"Anytime you want to, come back and skate," Page said. "You've got skating privileges. If I'm not around, tell anyone who asks that you have permission from Sol Page."

"Thanks," Curtis said. "I may take you up on it."

"You looked like you were enjoying it."

"I was. The pond is just like I remembered. The trees and the houses. The ice. It's a bit eerie after all this time. I sort of expected it to be different, to be changed. Like everything else. But it matched my memory perfectly. And how many things can you say that about?"

He had finished replacing his skates with his shoes, and slowly swung his feet into the car. He was ready to leave.

"Not many," Solomon Page said. "Not many things."

"No," Curtis agreed. "Not many things."

About the Author

During his career, Jefferson Flanders has been a sportswriter, columnist, and journalist, writing for newspapers, magazines, and the Web.

Flanders is the author of the critically acclaimed Herald Square, the first novel in a series about espionage in the early years of the Cold War.

www.ingramcontent.com/pod-product-compliance
Lightning Source LLC
Chambersburg PA
CBHW060621130626
46555CB00002B/597